Inside a pocket watch eye.

By Aaron Hodkinson

First Edition

Copyright © 2012 Aaron Hodkinson

ISBN: 978-1-291-23498-5

Printed and bound by Lulu.com

Cover design and artwork created by Aaron
Hodkinson

For my Parents and for Nic,
For always believing

Prologue.

Gideon Lilleyman sat slouched over his workbench in Lilleyman Clocks And Co. down Giggleswick Street in the town of Grimpo Grotton, he had been sat in the same position for the last three hours and had perused over the same map and documents for double that time. His fingers ran down the rough paper that must have been over two hundred years old and was definitely starting to show its age, the map showed Great Britain but a Great Britain that had much of the town that surrounded Gideon missing and in fact had most the major cities and towns missing which now sat dotted around 1883 Britain. Gideon murmured to himself as he looked in the dim light and was so engrossed in what he was looking at that he didn't even hear his apprentice enter the room, Takt Zifferblatt quietly walked behind his employer and casted his eyes over the hunched shoulders, Gideon had taken Takt in after he was orphaned some twenty years previous and since the boy then had no name to speak of, the clock maker decided on the name Takt Zifferblatt which of course is a strange name but apparently the clock maker had his reasons and Takt felt no need to argue, Gideon Lilleyman had been the best father the now twenty-five year old could have ever hoped for. "What are you doing?" Takt said quite loudly which instantly made Gideon leap off the small crooked stool he had been sat upon, "You scared me Takt! What are you doing creeping around at this hour?" said Gideon in a slightly angry tone that did not suit him, "I am sorry" he said "You just startled me is all, what can I do for you?" Gideon now asked more gently with a slight smile upon his thin face, he was a tall man with usually neatly sleeked back hair that now looked more ruffled with this late night, he had a thin black moustache that lined his upper lip and a gentlemanly posture, "I couldn't sleep, I was just thinking about what you had found" said Takt as he pointed his finger towards the work bench before stepping forward to get a better look, "I know, me neither, it is so exciting is it not? An object that possesses that much power and we have the map with the locations of the three fragments it is split into, the problem we have is where the actual locations are as this map, as you can see is extremely old" said Gideon as he looked back down at the map and pointed to different locations marked on it, "Do you have any idea where the pieces are?" asked Takt, "I do, the only way I know this is because I have found a book…" Gideon started as he reached under the workbench and pulled a large book from underneath, it was thick and black with very intricate designs carved into the cover, "I found it in the library as I was searching for information on anything that might aid me in my quest, it was lodged in between books about werewolves and books about witches which initially drew me towards it, what I found inside was incredible as it was full of scribbles and drawings of creatures that are apparently living amongst us, then I found this…" said Gideon as he thumbed to a page he had bent the corner of and pointed to a large paragraph that seemed to be mainly handwritten but in many different styles of writing which seemed to change as the writing moved down the page, much like the page had been added to and it had a drawing of a peculiar object that looked like an extraordinary clock, it had a jewel at its centre and had about six ornate hands that stuck out from a solid black face with silver gems that made numbers going from the number one, to the number sixty, "Is that it?" asked Takt as he moved closer to have a better look, "It is indeed, its states here that the Todesfall Clock, belonged to a powerful wizard who had created the clock in order to see his dead wife, but in doing so had opened a door to the world called the Malimar, it is said that this world is that of pure evil, it was created from the beastly and malevolent thoughts of man and had been contained but when Zaub

Hexenmeister the wizard, created the clock it was ripped into three pieces that became lost within the land and apparently fell into the possession of three different types of creature which unfortunately, are unknown, but as the clock was ripped into pieces the Malimar became open and the creatures within were free to roam our lands and have done so ever since but they are not always in plain view, some chose to influence the choices of humans without being seen and began to poison the Earth, but it states that combining the three pieces of the clock will close the Malimar doors and cast the creatures back within it" read Gideon and with that Takt stared at his father in astonishment, "Well, what do we need to do?" asked Takt, "Well, you are not going to do anything" started Gideon "Over the past few weeks I have researched where to find these pieces of the clock, I have also made a copy of the map and I intend on traveling to find them, you must stay here Takt, you need to continue working here and to not draw attention to my absence, if I succeed then our lives will change so much, I will be able to see my father and mother and you will be able to see your true mother and father, to see what they were like and to find out why they never named you" said Gideon, "But, I want to go with you" started Takt, "No my son, you must stay here, you must await my return, please do this for me" said Gideon as he started to rush around the shop collecting items and stowing them in a bag which he swung over his shoulder, "I must leave tonight as to not attract unwanted attention" he said as he grabbed a scroll from the side of the desk, he then rolled up the original map and notes, put them in an ornate box which had beautiful golden locks and ran up the stairs, Takt followed and when he caught up to Gideon who was now kneeling in the dimly lit living room on the first floor of the building, he was prizing a floorboard up and placing the box within the floor, "Keep this box safe, if I fail in my quest than I urge you to not follow in my steps and to always keep this box hidden in case anyone or anything comes to find it, please promise me this Takt" said Gideon as he placed the floorboard back and stood, he then placed two hands upon the shoulders of Takt, "Promise me Takt" Gideon said again, "I promise" said Takt, "Good, I am so proud of you Takt, you have become such a better man than I could have ever hoped for and I know you will lead a great life, but I must be going" said Gideon as he dashed out of the room, they ran down the stairs and Takt saw Gideon Lilleyman wrap his traveling cloak about his shoulders, tighten the strap on the bag that was fastened over his shoulder and then place a bowler hat atop his head, and before Takt knew it Gideon gave him a nod and exited the door before turning, running

back into the shop and wrapping Takt in
his arms, "Good bye my son" he said, "Good
bye father, take care of yourself" said
Takt and with that Gideon Lilleyman was
gone and what Takt Zifferblatt did not
know was that he would not see the man
that had adopted him and had taught him
the trade of fixing and building watches
and clocks for another one hundred and
thirty years.

1.

A Box of Clox.

Tick, Tock, Tick, Tock. This sound is a familiar sound within the shop walls of Pandora's Box of Clox, a crooked old building nestled between many other crooked old buildings down the dim and cobbled Giggleswick Street. This weary looking building belonged to Thaddeus Loveguard, the best clock maker and watch repairer in all of Grimpo Grotton, although he was well renowned his appearance did not reflect this, he was a shabby man with bushy hair which was streaked with grey like small lightning bolts on a jet black sky. His face was lined beyond his years and his chin held a permanent stubble, his eyes were blue but were so sunken into his weary face they seemed almost as grey as the streaks in his hair. His stature was average but seemed below this from the slumped over posture he had acquired, the clothes he wore were worn and tatty, stained with every type of stain you could think of and his shoes seemed barely able to cover his feet, looking as worn as the rest of their owner.

He wasn't old, he was in fact only thirty three but many people around the town of Grimpo Grotton mistook him for much older, It hadn't always been like this, but in a matter of fact Thaddeus Loveguard had not always looked so haggard and worn, it had only been in these last three years things seemed to go on a slight downward turn, since his beloved wife Pandora, had died.

Pandora Berrymay married Thaddeus Loveguard in the breezy spring of the year two thousand, they had known each other for 6 years before marrying but Thaddeus knew exactly at the moment he saw her that she will be the woman he married. The three years they were married were the happiest of his life, they did everything together even things that most people would see as mundane or even every day normal things would excite him just because he got to do it with his wife. They went places and had photographs to prove it, they talked all the time and were never annoyed by one another, they laughed together, smiled together and even eat pasta together. That was once, over three years ago and now the photographs seemed too painful to look at, his memories hurt him and what hurt him even more was the very fact that these memories caused him heartache. He missed her, every second of the day; she was the person that made him get out of bed in the morning.

When she was alive the shop was vibrant, the dust was absent, the tools were always polished and even the mat at the entrance to the shop was free of bits. Now, the shop was dull, the dust had made a permanent residence across the top of the shelves, the old clocks that hung crooked on the walls were now creaking, the mat at the shop entrance was full of dust and bits, the light that once seemed to radiate through the windows now seemed to miss out the shop on its daily adventure down old Giggleswick Street. The windows were cobwebbed and dreary, but Thaddeus didn't care, he didn't really care about much lately as his life was the same every day as he sat at the high, crooked workbench, the lamp bent over his head giving him sufficient light as he worked on an old cuckoo clock, the tools in his hand were rusted and well used, no longer clean and pristine like they were once were over three years ago. At this moment he looked up, the thought of her passed quickly as air through his head, she was still there reminding him to keep breathing.

He remained there, his bushy, scruffy hair dangling over his eyes, the tool he worked with being twiddled repeatedly in his hand. He looked down, and started to work again on the old clock, the cogs in the centre of the clock were well rusted which had corroded most of the mechanisms in the

old wooden shell, it was an easy job as
Thaddeus had many replacements for all
types of clocks, watches and even old
jewelry boxes with the tiny ballerina's
inside. This job would take him another
thirty minutes or so, he replaced parts
with great ease and was happy for the time
to do it as it occupied his mind in just
the way he wanted, he wished though that
he had a bigger project to work on in the
evenings as this was the time his mind
wandered the most.

He finished the clock soon after, placed
the backing back on the wooden case that
encased the clockwork, the familiar sound
of Tick, Tock resonated from inside the
old antique, he placed it back on the
shelf next to the other work he had
completed earlier in the day, the weight
of the clocks bending the old, black shelf
that was screwed crookedly into the dark
wall.

He glanced at the clock that sat just out
of his vision, the time read 23:28pm he
let out a sigh and began to stand, the
stool beneath him creaked with relief as
Thaddeus's light weight lifted off the
crooked seat, each leg seemed to have a
different length that sat at half the
height of Thaddeus, giving him the ability
to look down at the work he was involved
with, this gave him a hunched look to

anyone who would be peering in the few
clear patches of the windows.

He walked over to the shelf on the wall
closest to the old oak counter with its
partly dusty top, the only patches that
weren't dusty were where Thaddeus had
either been leaning or had placed a
newspaper or magazine. The counter top was
illuminated by a small lamp that was a top
the counter creating shadows throughout
the rest of the shop, clocks creating
shadows that drifted across the walls like
shy monsters and the cobwebs that seemed
hidden by daylight now became more
prominent as the night took over. He
looked around the shop from the counter,
thinking of many different things, his
mind wandering over the past years he had
spent alone here and with that he sighed
again and walked to the front door to turn
the Open sign to Closed then locked all
the of the rusty locks that were evenly
apart, starting at the top of the door
then to middle and the last being at the
bottom, they locked with a heavy thud and
clunk.

He turned and walked through the shop, not
looking around this time and continued
through the open door behind the counter,
closing the old and dirty looking oak door
behind him before continuing up the creaky
stairs to his flat above the shop.

Thaddeus awoke the next morning earlier than he would of liked, it took him a long while to arise from his crooked bed in his quite dreary bedroom, he sat up before long and gazed around, the bedroom he sat in was quite empty but had unusual character with the dark nearly black walls, the deep red curtains that were dusted and old and which ran down to the floor from near the cracked ceiling.

The wardrobe sat in the corner of the room, its weight had shifted to the left slightly over the years and now needed the wall near the window as something to lean on, much like a withered old man that had eventually had the age he was catch up with him. The door that led out of the room was crooked like nearly everything else in the building, if you were tall enough you would be able to peer through the crack at the top of the dark brown door, and the same applied for if you were the size of a mouse, as the bottom of the door didn't quite sit against the floor.

He stood and walked to the window while wrapping himself in his dressing gown; it was a deep blue gown with holes in the shoulders and a missing belt. The morning was bright but seemed gloomed in the dusty window, the sun shone down onto the empty backyard of the shop, behind that was a small walkway and then the entrance to the backyard of the shop on the next street.

He rubbed his eyes and walked to the glum bathroom, he brushed his teeth, attempted to peer into the dirty mirror but soon gave up. He didn't bother to brush his hair as he hadn't brushed it in the last two or so years, instead he just splashed his face with water and exited to get dressed.

Once dressed he stomped gradually back down the creaky stairs and walked into the shop, it was Sunday; he had forgotten this and a sudden dread of the possible emptiness of the day dawned upon him. It was the same every Sunday as he didn't have the distraction of work to fill up the empty hours.

He stood, rooted to the spot for what seemed like a long while but then he forced himself to walk over to the newspaper and glanced through it, he was bored already but then he spotted an advertisement about half way down the 7th page, it read:

CAR BOOT SALE

THIS SUNDAY

IN THE FIELD BEHIND THE OTHER FIELD NEXT TO THE BLIND WITCH PUB

SNODBURY STREET

9 - 7pm

Thaddeus thought for a moment, maybe it would be good to get out, well not good but maybe it would be another welcome distraction as after all he didn't plan on buying anything just to have a look around and then return to the dark and dreary shop where he felt safe.

He sat at the counter drinking his coffee, the handle on the mug was cracked and it was only a matter of time before the white cup with a spiral black and white pattern broke all together. His eyes glanced briefly over the pages of the rest of the paper but didn't rest on anything in particular, he noticed small snippets like something about a dog with a pencil for a tail and something about a woman who had lost her nine pet snails, but these were stories that gave Thaddeus no reason to carry on reading. He glanced over at the clock on the wall, **9:17am**; he stood, stretched, then closed the paper and placed it on the pile of other read papers at the side of the counter, the colors of the pages changing the more buried they were and gradually became a slight yellowish color, a gentle curve formulating in the center of the pile as the weight took its toll on the fragile paper. He picked up his now empty coffee mug and the plate that he had used for toast but was now empty all but from a few crumbs here and there, he walked through the open doorway into a small kitchen located next to the stairs that climbed to Thaddeus's flat above, he had started using this kitchen more and more over the last few months, it had once been empty with all his food still up in the rightful cupboards upstairs but recently things had started moving around, he didn't know why and put it down to himself mislaying things, until things he knew he hadn't mislaid ended up in different places, this didn't really bother Thaddeus that much as he always seemed to find the items that had been moved sooner or later.

He placed the mug and plate into the deep sink, looked out of the window to gage the weather before grabbing his coat from the hook hanging just at the base of the stairs. As he passed the counter quickly he went to grab his keys as he always did but-

They weren't there, where could they be?
He looked around quickly for the familiar
looking keys with the bright key ring
showing a bright star on a blue rubber
background, he had been given this by
Thelma Everthistle, the little girl that
lived with her mother Elspeth Everthistle
above the bakery across the street.

Just at that thought he saw a shiny object
hanging in the door, the door he rarely
uses his key to lock unless it is from the
outside, he walked to the door and surely
enough, hanging in the rusty lock were the
shiny keys with the familiar key ring
hanging next to them. Thaddeus swallowed a
little as he knew for sure that he had
left them where he always leaves them and
at that moment an unusual cold chill ran
up his spine like a snake that is made
from ice slithering up his back, he rubbed
his neck to relieve the chill and briskly
unlocked all the door locks, before
exiting quickly.

He inserted the key back into the door and
locked it with a single motion before
stepping backward onto the cobbled street
behind, looking up at the structure in
front of him, he suddenly realized how
unfamiliar it looked and as his eyes
reached the very top window, his very
bedroom, he saw a flutter in the curtains,
Thaddeus gasped to himself as it was not a
flutter that a breeze could of caused and

he knew that the window in that room was broken and could not be opened, This was a movement made from something in the room. He turned quickly and quietly, pushing his fists into the deep pockets of his long black coat, the cool morning air flowing over him like the very chill that had caught him at the door, the chill that had still not fully left him.

2.

A raggedy doll and an interesting idea.

Thaddeus walked along the cobbles, his feet tapping on the hard ground as he walked, there was no one else was around this morning, all the shops in the town closed on a Sunday which gave few people reason to venture out, the only people he did see on his walk were elderly people strolling arm in arm with their lifelong partners, the white hair of them visible from a great distance like small clouds but soon Thaddeus quickly caught up and then passed them effortlessly.

He turned down a dark alleyway that was surprisingly clean, much like the rest of Grimpo Grotten, large bins were strewn down the sides of the alley and so was the smell that oozed out of partly open lids. He was soon out of the alleyway and onto the main high street, but this was not his destination and he crossed straight over the large open path that was lined with designer shops and posh looking eateries, silver tables could be seen every now and again that accompanied the bistros and diners, warm smells floated around Thaddeus that could only come from the eating venues, some of these were open on Sundays but not for another twenty or so minutes.

Bright sunlight covered half of the large high street whilst the other half was cloaked in a still darkness that once entered gave the traveler a sudden chill that often made them shift quickly to the more appealing sunshine.

Thaddeus moved down a smaller street that had more cafes on each side, he kept walking down the cool street until he saw a sign in the distance that hung loosely from a decrepit looking building on the edge of a cross roads, it read:

THE BLIND WITCH INN

As he approached the closed pub, he noticed how old it really did look, with its cracked white paint around the windows and door, its worn looking brick work that made it look as if it would collapse at any moment, even the crooked roof looked as if it would slide right off the building, the doorway empty which made a change from the few times Thaddeus had passed the pub, the door was open and cackling could usually be heard coming from inside as well as the thick and unusual smell that oozed from the small pub. Thaddeus and Pandora had once ventured inside the pub many years ago, their stay was brief as the inside of the building matched the outside with its crooked walls that were a deep red color, the bar was black and dull, the glasses were tall and murky but what made the pair leave early were the people who were all slightly on the strange side, the women were cloaked with unusual features, some had long crooked noses with sunken eyes that never left Thaddeus and Pandora, they had long tangled hair and their long crooked fingers grasped the dirty looking glasses and Thaddeus was sure he saw one of the drinks in their hands start to bubble. The men were just as strange as their features almost matched the women in the establishment, they had piercing eyes that seemed bright blues or greens, their skin was pale and their features angular but they had more overt personalities than the women of the room, they sat with their chins high and in dark suits which still seemed dull and suited the room that surrounded them, the unusual men had long hair that was often tied back but some had it hang loose about their faces but whoever these people were they made Thaddeus and Pandora uneasy that day and a strange feeling had urged them to leave.

He rounded the corner next to the pub and crossed the road that was mainly busy around five o'clock on a week day as people left their places of work within the town. He walked a little before turning another corner towards a bright silver gate which had hung on it a sign that read:

CAR BOOT SALE

CAR ENTRANCE NEXT RIGHT

GATES CLOSE AT 7PM

He had made it; he nipped to the right of the gate to get passed and was soon stood at the start of a maze of cars and people with boxes and bags placed seemingly all over the large field. He realized that the noise of the area had suddenly grew whilst he was stood there slightly in awe, it was that of haggling regulars to car boot sales who were dressed in waterproof coats even with the sky now cloud free, their thin white hair floating a top their heads like small pieces of cobwebs.

There were of course, younger visitors to the event, people with small children that seemed overly excited at the sight of second hand toys for 50p that had an arm or leg missing, there were middle aged couples who wandered slowly through the maze and as they walked and talked they pointed at the items that surrounded them. There were people who held on awkwardly to pieces of furniture in fear that if they put the item down someone would snatch it from under their noses. Thaddeus walked forward slowly, glancing at the tables that sat behind open-booted cars with all sorts of interesting objects appearing to his ever wandering eyes, from desk lamps to shoes with missing laces and from wigs to kitchen ware with items having crudely hand painted signs stuck to them reading prices of all sorts.

Thaddeus gazed and occasionally gave a friendly nod to fellow car-booters who walked by him, he stopped at a few tables and looked at the mismatch of things, people who owned the items watched him like eagles, eagerly waiting for him to crack and buy something, but he didn't, he just gazed with a smile on his face but a smile that had been missing for far too long.

As he rounded the first corner of the maze he noticed something on the facing row of cars and tables, some shiny objects that seemed to attract him like a magpie and as he closed in on the table he realized he was in heaven, there littered in front of him were a dozen or so old clocks, some with hands missing, others with the cogs and mechanisms loose, some with just the face, hands and mechanisms but with no casing, he picked the relics up and examined them, they were in good condition a little worn here and there of course, but other than that they were all perfect.

He looked around some more before the owner came over, "Can I help you?" she said as Thaddeus gazed up to greet her, she was a small woman with curly shoulder length hair that seemed to cover most of her face as well as a pair of thick glasses that enlarged her eyes to double their natural size. She wore shabby clothes that seemed to be knitted together from other pairs of cast away garments, she looked somewhat like a patchwork quilt with glasses. Thaddeus glimpsed more of her face; she wore a warm smile underneath the hair which calmed Thaddeus slightly.

"Ummm yes, how much would you take for all of this?" replied Thaddeus in a slightly shaky voice, "All of it?" replied the woman with obvious surprise in her voice, "You must really like clocks" she said, the smile on her face growing even more, "I do, I own Box of Clox down on Giggleswick Street" responded Thaddeus as he looked back down to the mechanisms. He didn't mean to leave his late wife's name out when he told people where he worked, it was just a habit that he got from avoiding awkward questions about "how he is?" and "how is he doing?"

"Oh really, I know the place, I sometimes walk past there on way to my sisters on Bundlewick Street, I always mean to pop in as you 'av some wonderfully old and creaky lookin' clocks" responded the woman, her voice thick with a west country accent that made her even more friendly.

"Well 'coz I know they'll be goin' to a good 'ome , I can do 'em for £20 for the lot, 'ows that?" stated the woman as she looked at the items on the table, seeming to work out some form of sum in her head.

"That would be brilliant" responded Thaddeus excitedly; he quickly fumbled to get his wallet out of his pocket before handing the woman a crisp £20 note. "Would you like a trailer dear? Ya know, to cart 'em 'ome with you?" asked the friendly lady, "Do you possible have a large box? I don't live far away and I am used to carrying clock parts around" replied Thaddeus and just then he noticed something under the table that he hadn't noticed before, it was a raggedy old doll, it was ripped down the middle with its head hanging to one side, it seemed to be

made of the same material that potato
sacks were made of, its arms were missing
apart from some strips of fabric that had
once held some filling that occupied some
of the rest of the doll, its eyes were
once large but were now missing and he
looked very, very worn, it was something
that Thaddeus needed to have.

"How much more for the doll?" asked
Thaddeus without taking his eyes off of
it. "You want that? Why on earth would you
want a broken doll?" replied the woman
looking slightly confused but never losing
her smile.

"It is just part of a project that I am
undertaking" responded Thaddeus now
looking at the woman. "Tell you what then,
it's free to you, seeing as you gave me
reason to get off 'ome early" stated the
woman as she bent over slightly awkwardly
to pick the disheveled doll up off the
slightly wet ground.

She put it in the box with the rest of the
items that Thaddeus had purchased, as she
did this Thaddeus thought of the idea that
had sprung into his head almost as soon as
he saw the doll lying on the ground near
his feet. He would build the doll again,
place the clock mechanisms into the empty
body and build a clockwork boy, it would
never move he already knew this but it
would look impressive and would take up a

big part of the free time he dreads each day. He had many spare parts from the work he had done over the years that would be more than adequate for his project. Thaddeus felt excited as looked down into the box before him, a project he had craved for so long finally in his grasp, he smiled to himself and looked back up to the kind woman also standing before him.

"Thank you very much" was all he could manage to say. "You just take care of all of it" she said whilst smiling at him. "I will, I really will" he said as he picked the heavy box up but hid the strain that ran through him, excitement was more dominant in his mind at this point and he quickly started for the exit of the car boot sale. "Thank you again and goodbye" he called over his shoulder, slightly glimpsing the warm smile she had worn for all of their brief meeting as she waved goodbye to him.

3.

Something to build.

Thaddeus arrived back at Pandora's Box of
Clox quicker than he had thought, he
unlocked the front door and quickly
entered, closing the door behind him and
he placed the box of items on the floor,
locked the door again and pulled down the
dark blinds that hung above the windows,
dust sprayed down across Thaddeus's bushy
hair but he hardly noticed as he picked
the box back up and rushed over to the
work bench at the rear of the shop.

He turned both lamps on that gave him
adequate light on both sides of the large
desk, he then took the now buckling box
and emptied the contents on top of the
desk, taking care not to damage anything,
he took the ragged doll out first and
placed it to the side, he then placed the
mechanisms, cogs and clock parts neatly
together before disposing of the now empty
box that had transported his prized
possessions.

He looked at his treasures with a smile on
his face, then grabbed the old doll and
took it to the kitchen, taking a scouring
brush in one hand and a bottle of squirty

soap in the other; he began scrubbing and
squirting the soap on the tatty and
scuffed fabric, the dirt and years of
neglect seemed to wash away in the clean
water that spilled from the deep silver
tap. He scrubbed and cleaned and after
twenty-two minutes he had cleaned all of
the now soaked but happier looking broken
doll, Thaddeus smiled at it as he hung it
over a small maiden he had constructed out
of old television antennas for Pandora's
clothes a few years previous. The doll
hung their limply as it dripped water onto
a plastic mat that Thaddeus had placed
underneath to stop damage occurring to an
already damaged floor. He turned back to
the mechanisms that were strewn across the
work bench, taking a seat he took from a
small tub a blob of polish that would
restore the shininess of the cogs and
mechanisms. He then reached down to a
small shelf that he had built on to the
side of the bench that housed other
cleaning products like cloths and
toothbrushes, he had built many shelves
and storage areas onto the workbench over
the years which had seen it easily double
in size and was possibly the reason why it
seemed so crooked and why it seemed to
creak with every movement. There were
shelves built beneath knee level as well
as draws attached to the underneath of the
main table, Drawers and more shelves were
built onto the left hand side of the bench
while small cups had been attached to the

top end nearest the wall to hold paint
brushes, paints and glues, the lamps were
screwed down at the bases to prevent them
falling over while Thaddeus worked on the
various projects he had come in day in and
day out. Small diagrams and notes were
written on either small pieces of paper
that were completely selotaped down to the
table or written directly into the bench
as ideas or things that Thaddeus needed to
remember popped into his head.

He took into his hand a shabby looking
cloth before opening the pot of silver
polish, he then picked up a cog of
considerable size and took a pair of thick
lens glasses that had multiple lenses
attached which could be swiveled down to
improve magnification, the glasses were
gold framed but marked with paint and
pieces of glue that had been on Thaddeus's
fingers when working on previous projects,
the arms of the glasses were hooked behind
Thaddeus's ears and were hidden behind
thick hair that sprung out at different
angles. His glasses perched on the end of
his nose and magnified his eyes to
incredible size as he peered at the cog
piece; he reached up and re-angled the
lamp that was above and in front of him to
give better illumination. No other light
in the shop was on and it made the store
seem eerie even though it was only midday
but the fact that the blinds that were
covering the windows stopped most of the

light that was ever present outside from
penetrating through the thick fabric
strips. Thaddeus reached up without
looking and flicked a switch on a paint
covered radio that instantly sounded out
soothing violin music through slightly
crackling speakers, the feeling that
Thaddeus had felt a few hours ago when
something in his room made the curtains
twitch had all but disappeared, for now.

He began to clean the cog, starting in
small areas and then gradually growing in
the size of the circles he was creating,
the cog began to shine, the light
reflecting from it glistening upwards
towards Thaddeus, he cleaned more and more
and before long he had cleaned the entire
surface of the cog. He reached down to the
shelf at his side without looking and drew
up a small toothbrush with the bristles
worn and splayed, he began to dig the
toothbrush in between the small nooks and
crannies that the cog had, the corners
began to shine as much as the rest of the
mechanism and before he knew it he was on
to the next piece of tatty clockwork
mechanisms.

He worked tirelessly for the next few
hours, not really realizing the time but
he was enjoying himself so much that he
didn't really care, at around four hours
into his project he stopped to make a
sandwich in the dim upstairs kitchen,

quickly making it with a drink of orange
juice and bringing it back downstairs to
stand back from the workbench and look at
the work he had completed so far. He
smiled to himself, placed the empty plate
to the side and began working again, he
was good at working and he was always able
to motivate himself to complete a task he
enjoyed. Once seated again he took a small
screwdriver from one of the cups at the
head of the bench which held many
different sized screwdrivers as well as a
small hammer that had a small pot of nails
sat next to them. He began to unscrew the
hands from the clock face, then cleaning
the face before removing the numerals that
were situated around the edge of the white
disc, he put the empty clock face to one
side, and as he cleaned the hands he
looked at them carefully, they were
ornate, black and curled slightly at the
tips, they were long though and possibly a
couple of inches in length, he placed them
to one side and picked up another clock
face that was slightly more worn. He did
the same by removing the hands and placing
the face to one side, he did this for all
the clock faces until he had six hands all
cleaned and pristine looking, their ornate
lengths shining dully in the lamp light.

He continued working until the light
outside started to dim but by this time
Thaddeus had cleaned all of the
mechanisms, with the cogs and screws now

shining brightly and the clock faces were
stacked at the top left of the work bench
with the numerals and numbers placed in a
small pot that had been stored in a drawer
underneath the front section of the table.

He looked over at the now dry fabric that
hung on the maiden, he decided to wait
until the morning to start the piecing
together of his creation, he flicked the
switch which turned the lamps out, the
tools were ready for the next day and he
started up the stairs to the flat above.
He awoke the next morning with excitement,
he quickly got ready, pulling on clothes
from the crooked wardrobe and his shirt
was just as tatty as the day before with
small holes in the shoulders and rips in
the sleeves, paint speckled the front of
the shirt that had not come off in the
washing machine. He went through to the
living room and looked down onto the
street as he drank his coffee; the weather
was miserable which gave him all the more
reason to stay in and work on his project,
the street was damp and glistening with
the rainfall and the trickle of rain ran
smoothly down the crooked window as he
glanced across to the adjacent building,
it was very close and the window of the
building seemed close enough to reach
across to, the damp tiles of the rooftops
glistening just as much as the cobbled
street below. People scurried on the
street like small mice trapped in a

thunder storm, umbrellas, hoods and coats' covering the small people which Thaddeus thought to himself was a change from the car boot sale the day before where not a cloud had been visible.

He walked through the living room and into the kitchen, the kitchen that he used occasionally as well as the downstairs kitchen, he placed the used coffee mug into the sink without washing it. He quickly ran down the stairs filling the flat with the sound of creaks coming from every other step, he rounded into the shop, unlocked the door and turned the **Closed** sign to **Open,** secretly hoping that no customers would come in today even though he knew that Mrs. Bundleberry would be coming in to pick up her 80-year old clock that she had been given by her mother, and he knew that Mr. Oateymoore would be coming in later in the day to pick up his wristwatch. He went back to the bench and flicked the switch to turn the lamps on, illuminating the shiny cogs and clock pieces, he went over and removed the rags that were the old doll from the maiden and felt to see if they were dry which of course they were. He placed the doll onto the bench under the lamp light before sitting on the creaky stool and then started to examine the torn fabric, it would be a tough job but we was so excited to get started he quickly took a needle from a small case that was placed

on the left hand side of the pots that
contained his instruments of work, he then
reached over to the small box that was
screwed into the wall at the top corner of
the table, inside was a selection of
different color threads hung on small
wheels that were now warped with age.
Thaddeus didn't really know why he had the
thread as not many clocks needed it but it
just seemed to fit to have a selection of
threads attached to the massive work
bench. He licked the end of the thread and
slid it through the eye of the needle
before finding an area of fabric that had
been ripped apart, he pinched the two
pieces together and began to stitch along
the tear and before long had started work
on the next tear.

The door chimed with a ring as someone
entered the shop and sounded the small
golden bell above the door, knocking the
cobwebs and dust loose, it was Mrs.
Bundleberry coming in to pick up her clock
that had been sat waiting on the dusty
shelf above the counter for the last six
days. She walked slowly towards Thaddeus
with a slight smile forming at the side of
her mouth, she was a tall lady with a long
crooked nose and small beady eyes, but she
was friendly enough, her long dark red
coat nearly trailing on the floor as her
pointed black boots clicked and tapped the
hard stoned floor that was now covered by
small dusty rugs. Her long red nails

extending from her long crooked fingers
that were attached to slim boney hands
which protruded from the thick coat and
bent in front of her body like pale twigs,
her long black hair framing the rest of
her pale face like a dark shrouded web,
her head was held high as it always was
and seemed to peer down at most people,
this giving her a reputation for being
stern which Thaddeus knew was not true as
she was always very pleasant to him.

"Morning Thaddeus how are you?" she called
across to him as she walked across the
cold shop floor. Thaddeus looked up as she
approached with a small smile creasing his
face as he replied "Hello Mrs. Bundleberry
I am fine thank you, how are you today?"
Thaddeus stood and walked behind the
counter as she approached. "Oh I'm fine
thank you, I have just come for the clock
if you have possibly managed to finish it
yet?" asked Mrs. Bundleberry as she placed
her longer fingers on the counter opposite
Thaddeus, "Oh yes, I finished it just the
other day, here you are" Thaddeus stepped
up on a creaky old stool and grasped the
heavy clock with both hands; he gently
lifted it down and lowered it down onto
the counter for inspection.

"It looks perfect, just as it had done
when my mother gave it to me" stated Mrs.
Bundleberry as she looked around each side
of the now restored clock with amazement.

"It was no trouble at all, mainly just the cogs and paintwork that needed a little touching up and a little cleaning" replied Thaddeus just to fill the silence between Mrs. Bundleberry's gasps and quiet remarks on how the paintwork was "impeccable". It wasn't a difficult job for Thaddeus to complete as the design was very simple, a varnish finish with a glass front that housed the clock face inside. When Mrs. Bundleberry had brought it the varnish had faded, the ticks had stopped ticking and it looked its age but now it looked almost brand new with fresh ticking and a fresh coat of varnish. Mrs. Bundleberry didn't even look at Thaddeus as she handed him the money, the amount being the exact amount that Thaddeus had quoted for the work just over a week ago this being £45, people had told him he undercharged but the fact is the work he did wasn't hard, and it wasn't worth the money that people told him it was, not to him anyway but he was a hard worker and wanted to keep a stable business down Giggleswick Street, but at this very moment in the day all that Thaddeus wanted to do was to get back to work on his new project that sat sprawled over the workbench to his right and was illuminated by two lamps. Before long Mrs. Bundleberry was walking back towards the front door without even saying a word, apparently speechless at the sight of her newly restored antique clock, Thaddeus thought it was a slight over reaction but was grateful for the appreciation. As soon as the small golden bell over the door rang he moved as quickly as a mouse and was back to work on the clockwork doll that was coming along as well as he had hoped.

The doll started to take shape, the tears were sewn and the fabric looked clean, Thaddeus had started to piece the clockwork mechanisms together and had fitted the cogs together that made up most of the torso. He took the hands from the clock faces that he had dismantled the day before, he then attached them to thin metal rods which were the same length as the black ornate hands to make four fingers and two thumbs, soon the body of the doll began to take shape, the body made from cogs, ticking mechanisms that no longer ticked were installed into the torso, Thaddeus added wiring to the doll that held all the mechanisms and cogs in place, Thaddeus acquired the wiring from the small drawers and shelves that were attached to his work bench and were once part of old radios, television sets and other electrical equipment, Thaddeus wasn't the kind of man to through much away as he often thought that most things could be used again and this was a perfect example. Screws and small nails held the metal plating and mechanisms together and allowed the doll to begin to take a more human shape.

Thaddeus grabbed the fabric skin that
would incase the now completed clockwork
body and wrapped it around the figure,
lifting its weight slightly as he slid the
material underneath and sheathed the legs
before enclosing the feet, he did the same
with the arms and then with the hands, he
then reached over to the head that been
created separately, lifted it, and placed
it onto a small platform that would
connect it to the neck and torso area,
under closer inspection it would become
apparent that the platform was made from
watch faces that were either broken or had
just stopped working over time. Thaddeus
lowered the head down and screwed it in
before looking at the nearly completed
doll, he realized something was missing in
the face, he wasn't sure what though, the
face needed stitching up that was obvious
but there was something else, the face
looked vacant somehow but after a moment
of carefully staring at the doll the
answer came to Thaddeus, the doll was
missing a pair of eyes. He had been so
busy with everything else he had forgotten
about adding eyes all together; this was a
slight disaster he thought to himself as
he ran his now grubby hands through his
wild hair thinking of something he could
use. It quickly came to him after a few
minutes of contemplation, the old antique
pocket watches he had stored away in a
chest under the counter, he had been told

by Pandora that they would be valuable one
day and she was most definitely right.

He scurried to the counter and rummaged
under papers and books, "Advanced Clock
Making" read one book, "Cogs, Clicks and
Ticks" read another as he tossed them
aside, he found the chest hidden away in
the dark recess of the counter shelving
and he grabbed it with both hands, pulling
it quickly out from its dark haven before
dashing back over to the work bench. He
opened the already unlocked lid and gazed
upon the perfectly round, polished watches
but they didn't tick any more which didn't
matter as Thaddeus just liked the look of
antique and perfect watch making, the
golden edges gleamed in the lamp light,
the black hands stood perfectly still
under a pair of dust free lenses. He
gently lifted them out, one in each hand
and placed them on pieces of newspaper he
had laid out so they wouldn't get damaged
or even worse, get paint on them.

He grabbed smallest screw driver he had
from the work bench and took the back
casing of one of the watches off, this
would be the best way to attach them as
they would now have a completely flat
backing which would be easier for
attachment. Once he had removed the
backing from the second watch Thaddeus
carefully slotted the wide pocket watches
in position with surprising ease, it was

as if the openings in the clockwork head
wanted these particular watches to be used
for the eyes, he twisted the watches to
make them symmetrical to each other, once
they were both in place Thaddeus took out
the screwdriver he was using before and
screwed the watches to a piece of metal
that ran behind them, the holes for the
screws were luckily already created in the
metal from something it had once been a
part of, this made the eye attachment very
swift and easy. The eyes were attached and
finally Thaddeus lifted the fabric hood
that would enclose the head up and over
the shoulders, fastened the fabric at the
neck before he finally pulled the hood
over the face. He took out the needle and
thread and began stitching the loose ends
of fabric, he felt the dolls potato sack
skin tightening as he stitched each
precise stitch, he moved to the hands of
the doll that were long and spindly, he
tightened the screws around the fingers
but left enough room for them to
articulate, he stitched the fabric around
the wrists that covered the clockwork
internals of the arm. Thaddeus had fitted
a small antique steam pump within the
elbow that he had in his collection but
hadn't had a use for until now, in its day
it would have been used in a small boys
model railway but a few years previous the
obvious once boy but now man, had brought
the model railway set to Thaddeus and
seemingly gave it to him, stating he was

moving abroad and didn't want it anymore as well as refusing payment for it that Thaddeus had quite instantly tried to hand over. Thaddeus thought the steam powered parts would be a fitting use within the clockwork doll and had been right as they had fitted perfectly. He tightened the stitching at the shoulders and moved back to the neck, he tightened all the stitched joining around the doll before moving on to the ankles, feet and knees. He moved around the entire doll looking for splits or tears in the fabric and when there weren't any left he finally stepped back to admire his work. The doll looked fantastic to Thaddeus; the stitching was as good a job as he could have hoped for.

He looked around and realized that one of the clocks was missing from the shelf, it was Mr. Oatymoore's and when Thaddeus glanced at the counter he saw money had been left, he must have been so engrossed in his work he never heard Mr. Oateymoore come in and now he thought about it, it was dark outside. When he quickly glanced over at the clock on the wall above the work bench it read 1:32am, suddenly surprised at the time he darted over to the front door, locked it, closed the blinds and walked back towards the counter and work bench but as the thought of retiring upstairs to his bed came over him, he realized he didn't want to leave the doll at this pivotal point as he was nearly finished. He sat back down and pulled out his paint pots, he neatly painted the fabric around the mouth and also around his eyes, looking at it he realized it didn't need any more; it was perfect and looked perfect. The fabric was a lighter brown than the day he had purchased it, the pocket watch eyes shone in the lamp light, the zip mouth was partly opened to see a small amount of clockwork within the mouth, the slim but long torso held most of the clockwork and some of that was visible through the improvised stitching of fabric, cloth and leather that Thaddeus had attached due to the severe damage the doll had acquired. The legs were bound with old shoelaces which was tight and sturdy, the heart area of the doll was occupied by the largest cog that Thaddeus had in his collection and it shone in the light much like the golden borders of the pocket watch eyes, the long arms with long crooked clock hands and fingers hung lifelessly at the sides of the doll but its head sat staring straight at Thaddeus and in the face that he had created, he saw a friend staring back at him.

With his project now finished, Thaddeus now felt a little more complete and with that feeling he smiled at the doll and to himself as he sighed in happiness. He stood and walked backwards not taking his eyes off of the doll that stared back at

him through clockwork eyes, he didn't stop
smiling as he flicked the switch on the
wall and watched as the shop was
momentarily plunged into complete
darkness, but as Thaddeus' eyes re-
adjusted he could see the silhouette of
the doll sat atop the workbench and with
that he turned and made his way upstairs
to finally get some sleep.

4.

Takt Zifferblatt.

Thaddeus lay in his crooked and creaky bed
with a smile on his face, his eyes gazing
towards the cracked and old ceiling
without blinking. He lay there for a long
while just thinking of what he had
completed, it felt like a companion had
just been found, given a companion that
didn't move, talk or respond in any way
but that didn't matter to Thaddeus as he
was just happy to have something to look
at that was new and made by his hand. Then
the thought occurred to him, maybe it was
time for the Clock Shop to branch out in
to supplying something other than watches
and clocks, maybe toys would be a welcome
addition to the dark, crooked old shelves
that would bring in a few more customers
throughout the day, Thaddeus had enjoyed
making the clock doll and felt that he
could definitely make many more other
dolls for customers and children.

He decided then that the next day he would
scribble, write and draw some ideas that
could go into the shop to house the home-
made toys, just at that point Thaddeus
felt a chill run down his still form while
he lay there and it swept over him so

swiftly but in that brief moment Thaddeus felt terrified. Out of the corner of Thaddeus's eye he saw the heavy curtains flutter slightly as the chill brushed past them as well, at that point he remembered the sight he had seen as he set off for the car boot sale, the curtains of this very room fluttered in a room with no windows open, they fluttered just as they had done a moment ago, he lay there still as a pebble and didn't dare move, his ears pricking at any sound that may or may not of sounded, he suddenly felt very cold and very scared but he didn't move and as he lay there the crooked door creaked very slightly as though something had just brushed past it.

Then as suddenly as it had come, the chill disappeared and the warmth that occupied the room a few moments ago made a welcome return, Thaddeus finally relaxed and breathed out with relief but he still didn't fully trust the space around him as he felt someone was watching, but soon this fear left him as the tiredness that was looming in him suddenly made itself known and as he turned on his side, his eyes felt heavy and soon closed and before long his breathing became heavy with sleep.

Downstairs in the closed, dark shop there was not a sound present, the doll that Thaddeus had completed just a couple of hours previously sat lifeless in the darkness.

A creak sounded at the rear of the shop, the door that led into the kitchen moved slightly and a faint light sparked in the darkness, it was erratic in its movement and at first glance looked spherical in shape and light blue in color like a small ball of lightening that had been compressed and was hovering at about waist height. Under closer inspection it would become clear that it wasn't perfectly round at all but was a small ball of sparks that wiggled and sparked as it began to move slowly into the main part of the shop, small sparks shot out at different angles and lengths as it hovered and floated around the counter and the corners of the shop which were usually cast in shadow but now lit up briefly as the small lightening ball moved around the room, it flickered and flashed unexpectedly as it suddenly changed direction and now a faint sound could be heard but only very faintly, it sounded like tiny squeaks but as it moved around the counter and headed towards the work bench and closer to the doll the sound started to become more clear and now sounded like a small whisper, a whisper that sounded like it was being kept in a box or behind a wall, like it wasn't part of this world at all.

It hovered up the bench and started to spark more brightly as it approached the doll, a whispering that was once faint was now more prominent and sounded much more like a voice "Ah-Ha this looks extremely promising, thank you very much Thaddeus" the voice said as small sparks began flickering more brightly than ever, and then one of the sparks appeared like a tiny lightning bolt and shot towards the finger tips of the doll, briefly illuminating them before another bolt shot to the other hand, then two bolts shot to the tips of the feet, then a bolt to the head and finally a larger bolt shot straight into the chest and heart area of the doll. Small wisps began spiraling around the limbs and body of the doll which then seemed to… enlarge, the arms becoming longer as the mechanisms that were enclosed in the fabric grew, the screws and bolts becoming three to four times large maybe even bigger, the body becoming the size of around a 10-year old boy, the fabric not stretching but enlarging with the rest of the mechanisms and the pocket watches that Thaddeus had placed in the dolls head for eyes were now about the size of saucers.

Then the doll stood, not on the work bench but seemed to hover in mid air as it began to spin, then a faint ticking could be heard as well as the sound of churning cogs and rusted joints finally given the freedom to move, the large cog at the centre of the doll's chest began to twist and turn like it was finally a part of a large cog, steam puffed from the elbows as the arms moved and also puffed from the seams in the body as it came to life. The ornate clock hand fingers began to twitch with movement as the feet began to move gently, the hands now had more freedom and started to clench and release, then all of the small to large parts that made up the doll broke apart, the entire body came apart at the very same time and at that very moment all of the cogs, mechanisms, ticking parts and windy bits glowed with the same electric light that the lightening ball which hovered before the doll emitted. The room glowed electric blue as a bright light shone from the entire form of the doll. Then as quickly as it had broke apart, all of the now much larger doll pieces flew back together seamlessly, the fabric and metal parts not looking an inch out of place from what they were before, but now there was a renewed look to the doll, metal parts and ornate saucer-size pocket watch eyes glowed but the eyes seemed to glow an eerie green which was different to the rest of the body as that seemed to glow a metallic color, the doll now looked different, it now looked alive.

But then, after a moment of stillness the large, round clock-eyes swiveled slightly in the metal sockets, the hands moving around independently as the dolls head turned from side to side fluidly, it looked down at its clockwork arms and long, pointed fingers as it wiggled its now mobile legs and feet, its zipper mouth moved slightly and a small smile seemed to crease across the fabric. "This will definitely do" The doll said to itself, the voice sounding that of a young gentleman, but a gentleman not from this year, or maybe not from this decade due to the well spoken tone. "This will most certainly do, Thaddeus my friend, I owe you a great thank you" The doll murmured to itself with delight, it walked across the shop and towards the front door with small puffs of steam being pumped from the joints in the knees, elbows and neck, the steam followed close to the doll as it moved but soon disappeared into the air. The doll walked to the window and moved back the blind as it glanced outside, the light of the street shone onto the wide, circular watch eyes and at that moment they seemed more like eyes, the doll face having more of an expression than it had before as the area that held the pocket watch eyes widened and shrunk like real eyes, the fabric around them creased like that of eyelids and folded over the edges of the pocket watches. Where Thaddeus had painted faint eyebrows now looked more prominent as they rose and fell at the sight of new things and the mouth fell open in apparent shock at the sight the doll beheld out of the front, murky shop window.

He turned and started to walk towards the rear of the shop, he constantly looked at his hands and ran his metal fingers over his torso, he passed through the dark open door and looked up the stairs before starting to climb them, each step sounding heavier than he would have liked. He finally reached the top and stepped onto the landing with an audible creak, he looked around in the darkness before heading towards Thaddeus's room, when he reached the door he paused for a moment before gently pushing the door softly open, his clinking hands resting on the dull door knob as the old hinges creaked with the opening.

He looked over from the doorway as Thaddeus slept, his large round clockwork eyes glowing in the dark room, he walked towards Thaddeus apprehensively and as he approached the sleeping figure Thaddeus opened his eyes suddenly and stopped breathing, the now moving clockwork doll froze just a few feet from Thaddeus as they both stared at each other. Thaddeus screamed, his scream wasn't a proper scream as his throat was hoarse from being suddenly awakened, it was half a scream

and half a croak but his eyes spelled his
fear, they were wide and frightened as
well as being nearly as bright as the
doll's pocket watch eyes. He bolted
upright and scurried backwards, his bed
covers ruffling up as he moved as quick as
an insect across the crooked bed until he
fell off the other end. His body thumped
to the ground but his wild hair and
staring eyes could still be seen from
across the top of the bed, his scream had
subsided and had now been replaced by a
hand over the mouth and an arm extending a
pointed finger towards the still frozen
clock-doll. "Who? W-W-What are you?"
Thaddeus asked with a quivering and now
awake sounding voice, he didn't give time
for the doll to answer, "I'm dreaming,
definitely, I have been working far too
long on the doll and now I am dreaming
about him, it!, Ha Ha" he was looking
around the room frantically and looking
slightly crazed. A slightly confused and
also concerned look came across the dolls
face as he began walking towards Thaddeus
across the dusty bedroom floor, the small
puffs of steam floating close behind and
he looked as if he was going to speak, his
mouth slightly a gape with a raised arm
and a pointed finger, but Thaddeus didn't
give him the chance, "This is the result
of lack of sleep and eating cheese before
bed again" he murmured to himself.

The doll had reached him by now and was kneeling in front of him with a stream of moonlight that was piercing the room through the crack in the curtain illuminating the dolls face, in the light it looked almost childlike which seemed to calm Thaddeus for a moment, he stared at the doll with his mouth half open, the doll seized the opportunity, "I know this may be extremely difficult for you to comprehend but please, you must listen to me, I am real and this most definitely is not a dream" he spoke clearly as Thaddeus gazed back at him through the now clearing darkness. Thaddeus whispered something inaudible as the realization came over him that this might very well be as real as the room around him, something about the situation made him think this, it didn't feel like a dream as he knew dreams to feel mixed up and unusual even when recalling them the next morning. He looked at the doll and wondered how it could be but before he could think much more he spoke back at the doll, "Who are you? Where did you come from?" The doll smiled at him, the creases of the fabric around the old zipper mouth that Thaddeus remembered painting not that many hours ago folded in a seemingly friendly and warm grin. "My name is Takt Zifferblatt, you may find this hard to believe but I am a ghost, I have been haunting this shop for the last 125 years, I was a clock makers apprentice in a clock shop much

like this one, which was situated in the
very same place and was owned by Gideon
Lilleyman a great watch and clock maker
and who also taught me the trade before he
went missing in 1883, I then owned the
store for the following 5 years before
dying at the hands of a runaway carriage"
Takt looked slightly embarrassed, or as
embarrassed as a clockwork doll that had
been possessed by a ghost could look
before continuing, "I have been wandering
this building for over a century and have
seen many people come and go but when you
and your now late wife arrived I was so
reminded of myself and the clock master,
and so it seemed like fate when I saw that
you had purchased so many useful items on
your day trip to the field filled with the
modern vehicles that I couldn't wait for
you to finish, this" Takt said as he
gestured to his stitched together body,
"But then I was drawn to doll in an
unusual manner and before I could even
think, I had possessed it and I have never
felt so alive in all of my ghostly years".
Thaddeus looked on in amazement but
suddenly felt a sense of almost happiness
as he looked on at something so
extraordinary that a surge of excitement
ran through him. Before him sat something
he had created with his own hands and it
was alive, somehow it was alive and the
fact it couldn't be explained made the
whole situation even more exciting even if
this was all in his imagination he didn't

care, he finally had someone to talk to,
he finally had a friend, and this friend
sat in front of him in the most unlikely
of forms, the form of a ghost filled
clockwork doll that he had created named
Takt Zifferblatt, but come to think of it,
what sort of name was Takt Zifferblatt
anyway?.

5.

Under the floorboards.

"Takt Zifferblatt was the name given to me by Gideon who was like my father, I didn't know my real parents as I was orphaned at an early age but that didn't matter once I found my way to **Lilleyman's Clocks and Watches** as it was like my home from the very moment I entered, Gideon named me Takt Zifferblatt for some reason unknown to myself but if he thought it suited me I had no question against him" stated Takt as the two of them had moved into the living room which was lit by a single lamp in the corner, this illuminated the both of them as they sat opposite each other, Thaddeus was perched on the end of the worn looking and flat-cushioned sofa as Takt was sat opposite on a wobbly looking chair with his feet cradled on the wood that supported the crooked legs. "And you have just been haunting this building ever since your death?" asked Thaddeus curiously with his chin held in his right hand. "Yes, I have mostly stayed down in the shop amongst the old clocks, but to me the years passed so very quickly it was almost like a dream" replied Takt, "Does..Does my wife..? is she..?" asked Thaddeus with a quivering voice, Takt smiled and said "She isn't I am afraid but that is partly the reason I wanted to talk to you so greatly, you see, Gideon Lilleyman always talked about a clock of magical abilities, it was said that there existed a clock that could show you your long passed loved ones for a time, allowing you to receive some closure or some form of happiness, it was called the Todesfall Clock but was thought to be purely myth, Gideon however, thought differently and even had diagrams, sketches and descriptions of the pieces that were needed but he said he was passed on the information by a man he met whilst browsing at the town market, he quickly wrote down what he had heard when he returned to the store. The magical pieces are, according to the diagrams and scribbling I saw, scattered at 3 different locations". Thaddeus looked on in amazement and could barely speak but when he did he said "This is incredible and what is funny is that I believe every word, it is like I was meant to hear this, like we were somehow meant to meet, but where could the pieces of the clock be?" Takt looked on for a moment, no visible expression on his fabric and clockwork face before he replied, "Thaddeus, you have to understand something, since I died I have seen things, things that I would never have believed in my living life, but now I know there are things that dwell in this world that you could never comprehend" Takt's artificial face now looked quite stern or even quite afraid, "Like what?" asked Thaddeus now starting to become slightly afraid of something unknown himself, "As the world has become modernized, humanity have become blinded to the things that are much older than the race of man, there are creatures that you have only known to exist within fairytales and myths, it is my understanding that the clock pieces reside within the land around us, but in the clutches of creatures that, to the modern world, do not exist, it is with my help I believe that you could find the clock".

Thaddeus understood, which amazed him slightly, "Do you know where the plans and diagrams of the clock are hidden?" he asked, "I do indeed my friend" replied Takt "They are hidden under our very feet", he stated as they both looked down towards the dusted floorboards.

Before long Thaddeus had grabbed one of the screwdrivers that were in a small pouch that would sit around his waist but now sat at the side of his bed on the old wooden set of drawers, He grabbed the largest one with its deep red handle and deep shine of the silver metal, he quickly kneeled on the dusty wooden floor, the floorboards were out of line with small gaps formed between some of them. He jammed the screwdriver in between two

larger floorboards that Takt Zifferblatt
indentified as the right ones, Thaddeus
leant on the screwdriver, prizing it
upwards before it moved with some ease and
let out a creak of relief as it popped out
of place. Thaddeus pulled the entire
floorboard out and peered inside, Takt had
moved next to him and also looked into the
gap in the floor, Thaddeus then reached
into the hole and moved aside a thick
layer of dust that felt much more like mud
due to its amount. Under the dust was a
slight red color but something was buried
here, Thaddeus moved some more of the dust
apart until the golden shine of a latch
could be seen. Takt reached his clockwork
fingers into the hole and grasped the
sides of the now visibly rectangular
object, he pulled, and pulled, the object
didn't move so Thaddeus reached his hands
in as well and pulled, the object moved
under the force and soon enough the pair
were lifting a dust covered chest out of
the hole in the living room floor, it
wasn't big, maybe the size of a book and
the thickness of a brick but it had some
weight under it. They set it down on the
floor and looked at it, Takt reached
forward and placed a spindly finger into
the lock on the top of the ornate box, the
lock popped open and released, the golden
lock fell to the floor, knocking off some
of the thick dust that it had acquired
over the many years before revealing an
ornate and interesting pattern around the

lock area, this being that of crooked golden fingers holding the lock in which a large key may fit, around the pieces that wrapped around the chest looked to Thaddeus to be branch like with large golden leaves protruding from them. Thaddeus didn't have the time to look long as Takt was already opening the chest, the dust falling as the hinges creaked open and as the lid fell open the pair gazed into the old chest, inside sat many small pieces of paper that had unreadable scribbling all over them, Thaddeus rummaged through the papers before he finally saw something of interest, there seemed to be a larger piece of paper that had a form of drawing on it. "What's this" asked Thaddeus curiously as he unfolded the paper, inside there seemed to be a map, Takt looked over at it, "That's the map, the map which tells you the locations of the clock pieces" spurted out Takt as his face seemed to show a form of excitement. "It looks like the locations are all over, the country?" asked Thaddeus as he turned the map in different angles to make more sense of it, "That sounds right, I remember Gideon saying the very same thing" replied Takt as he looked like he was expecting the very news, "There seems to be one in the top, north area of Scotland, then another in North Wales, and then the last in the very center of the country, maybe towards Birmingham I can't be sure as this map is very old" stated

Thaddeus while he pointed to different points on the map that had either a star or a star shape scribbled next to locations that were written onto an extremely old looking map of the United Kingdom, the paper had become yellow in color, the ink had become dull with a list of different notes running down the right side of the map under a very detailed drawing of a compass. The list included many different items and notes which rained from things like: *Black Glasses, a small taste of black moss (for the shrinking), be careful of the pixies*. To Thaddeus this was a bewildering list of notations that made no sense at all but as he glanced over to Takt who was now peering over his shoulder at the large map, there was a look of remembrance on his fabric and clockwork face. Thaddeus understood there would be things he may encounter that he wouldn't understand but would have to in order to get the pieces of the Todesfall Clock.

Takt Zifferblatt reached into the open chest and took out a piece of paper that been bound and folded, as he opened it the pair saw small writings covering the pages, as they read it seemed to be a list of checkpoints or even directions that didn't seem to be completed, "It looks to me that we may need to find our own way at some parts of the journey" said Takt just loud enough that Thaddeus could hear,

"What do you think "Man of the Corn" means?" asked Thaddeus as he stared at the very first direction that read:

"Man of the corn can show the way, he is wherever you need him to be, just look for the corn and the way will be shown".

"I have heard of Man of the Corn, he is said to dwell within corn fields but can travel between any cornfield within the world, he is a gatekeeper of sorts and I believe that cornfields are gateways for mythical creatures, but these creatures need guiding in their travels, and so the Man of the Corn is always there to guide them." Replied Takt confidently. "Sorry Takt" started Thaddeus nervously, "I hope you don't mind but how do you...?" stated Thaddeus before Takt politely interrupted "How do I know so much about these things? I knew you would eventually ask this, and to be honest the answer is quite easy to explain, since I died, my mind has become more attuned to the supernatural world, my eyes are now able to see what dwells within the land and I also have an unusual knowledge of who and what different creatures are, I suppose it is due to my "unnatural" self, but you will also be able to see the hidden creatures the more your mind becomes open to this other world" The pair looked at each other for a long moment before Takt looked down again at the small booklet of scribblings, "I think I see the first destination Thaddeus" started Takt as he pointed a finger at the paper, Thaddeus looked down and noticed a small circle next to the first destination and when he looked across at the map he noticed the same circle around the same place that Manchester would be. "It looks as though Gideon made a key" stated Thaddeus as he glanced between the rough edged paper and the large map with the paper illuminated by the lamp. "I think your right Thaddeus, I think these written documents by Gideon may lead us to where we need to go, maybe this was his way of hiding his discoveries in case someone were to find the chest" agreed and stated Takt as he looked closely at the map. Takt looked up at Thaddeus with happiness, "Will you come on this adventure with me Thaddeus, I believe it to be our destiny" asked Takt hopefully, Thaddeus looked from Takt Zifferblatt to the map and back again, his eyes showing his thoughts all too well. "I too believe it to be our destiny, I am lonely here, I think you coming to me was a sign, or fate or, something, I'm not sure what, but what I do know is that I think I need this, I think I am ready for an adventure, let's do it Takt, let us find the pieces of the Todesfall Clock" responded Thaddeus as his voice seemed to become louder with each word, with each word Thaddeus knew more certainly that he would do this, and he knew then that this adventure may be the thing that would change him forever.

6.

Stepping into a new world.

The clock said 8:23am through a thick layer of dust that covered the red numbers that stared back at Thaddeus as he opened his eyes, he hadn't slept much, the excitement and anticipation about the coming day was overwhelming him. He rolled over onto his back and stared at the familiar spot on the ceiling, he had only been lying in bed for the past three hours and he and Takt Zifferblatt had been talking far into the night about the plan for the following day. Thaddeus shifted and looked towards the window and saw Takt sitting in the old arm chair in the corner of the room staring back at him, "Morning Thaddeus" said Takt cheerfully, Thaddeus groaned as he sat up in bed, "Morning" he replied with a hoarse voice that took him slightly by surprise. He shifted again before moving to the edge of the bed, placing his still socked feet on to the dusty floor, and then stood, his body felt weary from tiredness. "I packed some things in your satchel for you, some clothes and a little food that I got from the kitchen, are you sure you still want to do this?" stated Takt as he to raised to his feet and looked over at Thaddeus,

Thaddeus looked over at his shoulder towards Takt, a small smile creasing his face making it more lined and crinkled than usual, "More than anything" he replied "Thank you for packing my things, I don't have a lot but I know I can't wear the same old tatty clothes every day" chuckled Thaddeus slightly to himself, he moved over to the bag, picking it up he looked inside and smiled again, "To be honest, all my clothes seem tatty" Takt Zifferblatt laughed with Thaddeus as he walked over to join him. In the front pocket of the worn satchel sat a few items of food, two bottles of **Springing DettiFossy Falls Spring Water** and a few bags of crisps that Thaddeus had been saving but thought this was the best time to use. In the main compartment of the satchel lay a few shirts and two pairs of jeans that were neatly folded, the satchel also included a shirt that Thaddeus had forgotten about with its black and white stripes and a ripped front pocket. There was also a tatty old woolen hat which would cover most of Thaddeus' head when it was snowing in Grimpo Grotton's cold winters and there was a scarf that was just as worn and tatty as the wooly hat lying next to it.

Thaddeus walked to the bathroom, he didn't look in the mirror this time and instead just splashed his face with water, brushed his teeth and then took the toiletries into the bedroom and shoved them into the rear pocket of the satchel, he looked around and saw that Takt was no longer in the room, he glanced behind him and before long heard the sound of clinking metal coming up the stairs. Takt walked into the room holding a cup of tea that was steaming hot, the steam raising into the room with curly wiggles, the heat radiated from the cup as Thaddeus thanked Takt and took it in his hands, he blew and sipped at the hot tea as he looked around the room, Takt didn't need to ask what was running through Thaddeus' mind as he already knew. Thaddeus gazed at the old crooked furniture, the wonky wardrobe that leant into the crooked walls and the crooked bed that stood atop four crooked and curled legs which didn't seem able to support the weight of it. Thaddeus looked over the rest of the room, his eyes drinking in the memories as his mouth drank in the rapidly cooling tea, would he ever see this room again? What would the adventure they were about to embark on have in store for them? Thaddeus' thoughts returned to the present as he looked over at Takt who sent him a small smile, "I'm ready Takt, let's go" stated Thaddeus confidently as they started for the stairs, the satchel that Takt had packed was strapped firmly across the Thaddeus' shoulders as they stomped down each creaky step, Thaddeus did not dwell on past memories for too long as he realized they

were becoming quite painful at each
thought of leaving Box of Clox for an
unknown amount of time.

The pair looked quickly around the dusty
shop for anything extra they could take
with them, Thaddeus took the small belt
off the work bench that held different
tools such as a selection of screwdrivers
and a small hammer, even though he wasn't
sure when he might need these tools but he
felt that having them was like having a
piece of the shop hc had dwelled within
for the past years.

They started towards the door, the
excitement in Thaddeus had now started to
disappear as he became scared of the
unknown, he looked into the satchel again
and saw the diary snippets and maps with
the lists and diagrams that Takt had
stuffed into the back compartment that the
toiletries sat in. They reached the door
and unlocked it, Takt placed a sign in the
window that read:

Closed for a well deserved holiday...

The sign was written crudely by clockwork
hands on a small, yellowish piece of paper
that was creased and had tears in the
corners, it hung loosely in the window so
it could be read by possible customers.
The unlocked door opened at Thaddeus's
touch and Takt placed an old hat on his
head that belonged to Thaddeus, he wrapped
himself in a three-quarter length coat to
hide his appearance as the pair stepped
over the threshold of the shop, they shut
and locked the door behind them and turned
to walk away. Thaddeus looked back at the
shop, the windows dark with his absence,
he sighed and smiled before turning to
walk down the cobbled streets of Grimpo
Grotton, the outcome of the journey ahead
of them unknown, he was excited again; a
smile creased his lined face for the
second time that day.
They walked down the cobbled streets, Takt
held his collar high over his face and had
the hat pulled down to cover most of the
upper part of his face, he had slipped
some old shorts of Thaddeus' on and was
also wearing an old pair of trainers that
were worn and scuffed, he blended in well
enough and whenever someone did pass the
pair they didn't even look at them twice.
Thaddeus and Takt rounded a corner and
then crossed the nearly deserted road,

their destination was the train station, there they would analyze the map and list of destinations that was held within Thaddeus' satchel hung tightly over his shoulder. They walked down a lengthy lane, past numerous shops and stalls that were slowly being opened, Thaddeus rarely looked into the shop windows but when he glanced at Takt Zifferblatt at his side he noticed the gleam of his clockwork eyes and noticed he was looking around in wonder, Thaddeus thought to himself if Takt had ever been outside when he was in his ghost form, was this the first he had seen of the modern world since his death over a hundred years ago?. They kept walking and soon the sign for the train station became visible, they crossed the road again and were soon entering the station.

It was dim within the wide building, the lights were low but the familiar noise of the train station was ever present, the horns of trains arriving and departing could be heard through long echoes, Takt and Thaddeus walked over to the counter which was situated in a dark corner with a large clock above it, the hands were curled and the frame to the face was just as curly, the framework was dark green and even over the noise of the station a loud ticking could be heard as the pair approached it. A small huff of laughter could be heard as they both noticed the

clock, they looked over at the same time
to their right and noticed a homeless man
laughing at them, he had a long curled,
grey beard and was wearing tatty brown
clothes with a long black scarf that could
have been any color, but it was so dirty
that it had a black sheen to it, he had
fingerless gloves, one of the fingers was
raised pointed in Thaddeus and Takt
Zifferblatt's direction. His laugh was
cackled and hoarse, his dark eyes were
wide but slightly hidden under bushy and
wild eyebrows, he had long scruffy hair
that was poking out from underneath a
ripped wooly hat, not too dissimilar than
the one that was in Thaddeus' satchel. The
man kept laughing before shouting "I know
what you're looking for, you won't find
the pieces, and you won't win!" Thaddeus
looked down at Takt who looked a little
startled at the man, "Don't worry about
him, he shouts at everybody who walks past
him" Thaddeus told Takt but he didn't
respond right away, "Takt?" asked
Thaddeus, "Sorry, it's just that man isn't
who you think he is, he is a Domovoy, but
to you he looks normal" stated Takt as he
looked back up to Thaddeus, "What is a
Domovoy?" asked Thaddeus sounding slightly
confused. "A Domovoy is part of the spirit
world, a hairy demon-like ghost that
dwells within urban areas; it is partly in
the human world and partly in the world
called the Malimar, it is where evil
lives, notice how the light around him

seems to be non-existent, it is dull and dim around him" Now that Thaddeus looked he did notice an absence of light, there was a sense of something not quite right about the man sat in the corner, and when Thaddeus thought back he realized that he always felt this unusual feeling when he saw the hairy, bearded man.

"We have to get away from him, he is dangerous to us and we also do not want to draw attention, I will tell you more when we board a train" Takt said eagerly and Thaddeus agreed strongly as they hurried towards the desk that was fronted by a high window, behind of which sat a little old man with a bald head and small oval glasses, "Two tickets to Birmingham please" asked Thaddeus as he fumbled with his wallet and slid a ten pound note through the small gap in the glass, it seemed so natural to say the destination even though Birmingham was in fact not their destination just yet. He knew this from the directions that were scrawled across the old paper in his satchel, he had memorized the locations they needed to go the night before, they were strange but Thaddeus didn't question it, as the first place they needed to go was a corn field just outside Bristol.

The old man behind the glass didn't speak but instead just slid the small train tickets back through the gap in the glass.

Thaddeus took the tickets and beckoned Takt to follow, to the ordinary eye Takt looked like a teenager, wrapped half in winter clothes with an old three quarter length jacket on, but there were much stranger fashion trends wandering the streets of Grimpo Grotton. As Thaddeus and Takt climbed the stairs that led to the bridge which would take them across the tracks and down to their platform, Thaddeus took an opportunity to glance back at the homeless man that now turned out to be a form of demon ghost, he saw him still sat in the place he was a moment ago, but he was no longer laughing or pointing but now he was just staring, staring right in their direction. Thaddeus felt a chill and hurried their pace across the bridge and soon they were stomping down the next flight of stairs which ended on their platform.

They didn't have to wait long before their train came storming into the station and to a shrieking halt right in front of them. The doors slid open with a beep and the pair were soon boarding, allowing them to find a seat, there were many available as it was still reasonably early in the morning and not many people had a reason to board a train to Grimpo Grotton. They sat at the rear of the train, Takt sat closest to the window and Thaddeus slumped next to him which stopped any passing passengers from getting a good look at the

clockwork man or what the pair were
looking at.

No sooner had they sat down that Thaddeus
brought the satchel to his lap and took
out a selection of papers that had the map
and locations with item descriptions
untidily scribbled onto them. Thaddeus
looked over at Takt who looked right back
at him, "There is a different world out
here Thaddeus" Takt began, and Thaddeus
placed his head against the headrest
listening, Takt was good at knowing what
to say, he seemed to be able to know
exactly what Thaddeus was thinking and was
able to explain anything he was wondering
about, but then Takt continued, "There are
creatures, many different creatures that
we may encounter along out journey, some
are good and have always been good whilst
others are evil, your mind must be open to
this Thaddeus, believe what is out there
and you will see it also, the fairytales
that children are told have origins,
origins that come from these creatures
which were once the main occupants of the
lands and when man came, they hid or
blended in to their surroundings whilst
others have found ways to live amongst
humans, and not all of them are good, some
are purest of evil just like the Domovoy
we saw before", Thaddeus felt another
chill at the name, he hoped never to see a
Domovoy again but had a feeling that his
hopes may not come true. The train lurched

forward as it started on its journey and with that Takt Zifferblatt continued, "One of these creatures has even entered your shop once or twice" with that last statement Thaddeus looked over at Takt with a shocked expression on his face, "Who? I have never felt any sense like I did with the Domovoy" but Takt interrupted, "The creature wasn't evil, she was just living her long life, it was Mrs. Bundleberry, and she was a Spindlebock which is basically a spider, she actually has eight legs but conceals them within her dress, her true form is somewhat like that of a dark green spider crossed with a human, her hands are spindly and she can spin webs which she would do within her home" and with that Thaddeus remembered her appearance but not only that he started to understand, to realize the world he lived in and the world that was intertwined with his, like a large plant that needed his world to survive, but he could hear Takt speaking again "We will encounter more creatures and by the look of the maps and notes we have, we may encounter some sooner than we think, at our next stop we must travel to the corn field, that could only mean that we have to visit the Man of the Corn, I heard Gideon mumbling about a man called Manni Mais who is the gatekeeper and should help us on our journey". Takt Zifferblatt rifled through the papers with his long fingers, the now much larger

clock hand fingers passing through each
page with ease and his large pocket watch
eyes glancing at the notes with quick
agility.

Thaddeus placed his head back against the
seat and looked ahead as his mind
wandered, the sound of paper being handled
was clear next to him but soon started to
fade as he thought how his life was going
to change, would he ever see the cobbled
streets of Grimpo Grotton again? What
about his crooked shop that he had spent
so many years? His mind then turned to
Pandora, what would she say if she could
see him now? Sat on a train with a ghost
that had inhabited a clock work doll he
had made, a doll that had enlarged itself
and had now convinced him to go on a
journey to find pieces of a clock that
could allow you to see your departed loved
ones again, if only for a short time, a
journey in which he would encounter
monsters and creatures that were only
known in the dusty pages of old fairytale
books.

As this thought passed through his head,
he felt something familiar, it was the
excitement he had felt the night before
and with that he smiled to himself as he
closed his eyes, he needed as much rest as
he could get before they reached their
first destination, the corn field and the
Man of the Corn.

7.

The Man of the Corn.

The train came to a halt, a halt that
awoke Thaddeus from a near deep sleep and
as he glanced around he saw Takt
Zifferblatt already with the scruffy coat
and hat wrapped around his clockwork body,
"Are we here?" asked Thaddeus sleepily,
"We are indeed well, as close as we can
get to our destination, you have been
asleep for a couple of hours" replied Takt
cheerfully and with that Thaddeus realized
that the clockwork man who was stood there
in front of him probably didn't sleep,
ever. Thaddeus stood and grabbed his also
scruffy coat from the over head shelf, he
slipped it on as the pair walked to the
nearest door and waited for it to open, it
wasn't long before the familiar beep
sounded and the doors slid open
effortlessly, the pair stepped out and
down onto the platform, a cool chill
breezed past Thaddeus' face as he pulled
his collar up slightly and looked up and
down the platform, "Where to Takt?" asked
Thaddeus as he glanced over his shoulder
towards his companion, the dull afternoon
light shone brightly out of nearly
concealed pocket watch eyes. "We need to
get to Barking Hollow Farm on Grover Road"

said Takt as he glanced at the list of
locations and directions that were grasped
in his long fingers.

A few moments later the pair had jumped
into the back of a taxi, they made sure
there was a seat that faced away from the
driver so Takt could sit without the
driver noticing his clock eyes, and before
long they were on their way with the
driver luckily knowing exactly where their
destination was, even though he did have a
slightly puzzled look in his eyes as he
realized they didn't really look the
farmer type. He was a large man with a
large thick black moustache, his hair was
thinning on top and his shirt was a dark
blue color with some staining from
whatever he had for dinner. His eyes
constantly glanced back at the two sat on
the slightly smelly seats and Thaddeus
made sure they didn't speak of anything
that may draw more attention to them and
sat the entire journey in silence. Soon
the road in which they were travelling on
became more bumpy, the smooth tarmac had
turned into muddy potholes with a thin
wire fence that lined each side of the
trail, beyond that were fields and beyond
that was a line of tall trees, but soon a
farm came into view, it was a large
building with many other buildings
surrounding it, they soon came to a stop
not too far from the large farm. Thaddeus
paid the driver and stepped out of the cab

which soon started to move away, the sound of the grumpy engine traveling down the bumpy road gradually started to fade and before long the pair stood alone in front of a gate that had an old sign with red painted lettering on it that read "Barking Hollow Farm" and beyond that there was a faint yellow glow, it was the corn field, their first destination.

They didn't want to draw the attention of the residents of the farm so instead they snuck along the side of the small wiry fence that lined the perimeter of the land. Thaddeus could feel his worn shoes getting soggy with the mud that was starting to swallow his feet with each step, there were small bushes next to them as they walked, the faint smell of lavender and other herbs filled Thaddeus' nose, he wasn't even sure if Takt Zifferblatt could smell and thought it may be rude to ask. Soon they had traversed over the small herb patch and were at another fence that went in another direction for as far as Thaddeus and Takt could see; they followed it back towards the farm, crouched down as much as they could without falling over. The mud wasn't as thick here, it had more grass sprouting from it and also had a harder feel under foot, before long they were behind the farm buildings and stood at a large metal fence that separated the farm and the cornfield they needed to reach. They stood for a moment, then looked at each other, "Is this definitely the place?" asked Thaddeus glancing towards the field with its high spears of corn that stood much higher than Thaddeus "I am most certainly sure, Thaddeus" replied Takt as he looked ahead before stepping a foot forward, Thaddeus followed and they were soon past the metal fence and entering the cornfield, the stems of corn looked even higher as they approached and before long they were soon surrounded by them, they could not see where they had entered from and soon seemed to be lost in the vast field. They seemed to walk for a very long time without any real knowledge of what they needed to do, Takt referring to the directions he still had but were now being stored in the jacket pocket that he wore. The old papers didn't reveal any ways in which to further their journey from the cornfield or how to contact the Man of the Corn; it just listed the locations in which they needed to travel to.

But just as hope started to fade from Thaddeus he saw something up ahead, it was a silhouette against the light a head, a thin silhouette that seemed to be some sort of post or small spear in the sky, but it was moving, moving towards them. Thaddeus placed a hand on Takt's shoulder to stop him in his tracks, Takt looked up and saw the object in which Thaddeus was looking at, it was still unclear in what the object was but now a noise could be heard, a rustling sound coming from the direction that the tall object was situated. The corn started to move ahead and the sound of someone or something moving closer filled Thaddeus' ears, the pair stood very still and waited, they didn't know what they were waiting for and couldn't move from the spot they were rooted to, had the owners of the farm seen them? Were they coming to find and possibly shoot them on the spot? But soon a small figure could be seen, a dark figure that was approaching through the corn and before long a small man came shifting through the towering corn in front of them. His hand grasped around a tall staff that was carved with intricate leaf patterns, it seemed too tall to be able to be moved with one hand but the man in front of them seemed to do it with ease and without seeming to have the need to lean on it very much. "I know why you have come here Thaddeus Loveguard and Takt Zifferblatt, the question is, why it took you so darn long?" the old man said with a small smile creasing his face. His skin was leathery and oak colored and his head was bald and so shiny that it seemed to reflect the sky above. His beard was the longest, whitest and curliest that Thaddeus had ever seen, his clothes were farmer like, worn and weathered and his skinny limbs poked out of his clothes like the very corn that surrounded them. Snails slimed across the worn clothing and were seemingly coming from a basket the old man was carrying, the color of the basket blended to the corn field they stood in, it was light brown and made of a wicker material but seemed old, the handle in which the old man was grasping seemed very ornate with the same type of pattern carved into it that was on the staff grasped in the old man's other hand. The basket was full of snails in fact, all different colors, sizes and shapes and some Thaddeus had never even seen. They moved slowly within the basket, the ones that were on the man seemed to not be moving and were perfectly happy to have a better view from the old man's now slightly bent back. He wore a pair of loosely made sandals that strapped across his boney feet that were a deep brown color and were crusted in dried mud; he didn't seem to be a heavy man as he wasn't even leaving footprints in the loose earth.

"Ah, you have noticed my snails" said the old man, "I like to collect them, from all the fields I visit" he chuckled. "They are so different to any snails I have seen before" said Thaddeus still gazing at the basket. "They are very different, and the fact that you can see them for what they are means that your mind is changing" said the old man with a small smile on his face, "What do you mean? My mind isn't

cha…" Thaddeus stopped speaking because at
that very moment something happened within
the basket, the snails began to stir and
then their very shells began to move, they
uncurled and unfolded and twisted into
different shapes, wing shapes in fact and
as the uncoiled they showed the colors of
indescribable brightness, reds and blues
with shining silvers, pinks and purples
with a seemingly neon glow running through
the centre of the wings. Their bodies
changed color too, they were no long a
deep green color but were now all
different colors and in fact they kept
changing color Thaddeus noticed, as the
light caught the small bodies through the
tall corn, the snails seemed to turn
different shades of light purple, blue and
pink and at that very moment they took
flight. The snails lifted out of the
basket and off of the back of the old man,
they fluttered around his old bearded face
leaving trails of small wisps of colorful
mist, they then fluttered between Takt and
Thaddeus, the noise was that of a light
humming and it sounded like a warm breeze
blowing around Thaddeus' face and filled
him with happiness. He felt different as
well, as if the adventure they were on was
his destiny, he could see images in front
of his eyes beyond the brightly colored
now flying snail wings, he knew this was
real, that what they were doing was real
and he felt more alive than ever. He heard
a whisper in the fluttering wings, a light

voice and a voice he hadn't heard in the last three and a half years, it was Pandora's and even though the words were inaudible, he knew what she was trying to say to him, she was saying she was proud of him.

And with that the fluttering stopped, the small snails took off into the air and the light from the sun shone onto Thaddeus' face as he tracked the flock, they disappeared into the bright days sun, what was once a dull day had now become a cloudless afternoon. Thaddeus smiled to himself and looked at Takt Zifferblatt who was smiling back at him, Thaddeus wondered what Takt had seen if anything but Thaddeus felt the need to look towards the old man in front of them who was also smiling, "What were they?" asked Thaddeus, "They are called the Sidhee, they are a type of fairy and have been with me for a millennia" replied the old man who was now gazing skywards, "But you said you collect them?" asked Takt, "Oh but I do, I find them on my travels in different corn fields, but I must admit, I haven't managed to find any in the last three thousand years". For a reason beyond Thaddeus, he wasn't at all surprised at the age of the old man before them; Thaddeus was already beginning to understand this other world he was getting a glimpse of. "How do you know the Sidhee want to be with you?" asked Thaddeus,

"Because I am their maker, I plant small snail shells within the cornfields and after one hundred years, the shells hatch and the Sidhee are born, but after a hundred years I sometimes forget that they are ready to hatch and it takes me some time to locate them again" chuckled the man who's laugh was as creaky as an ancient forest tree. At that point Thaddeus glanced up at the staff the old man was still grasping tightly, a few feet above the tops of the corn there were multiple signs pointing in different directions from the staff, the only lettering that Thaddeus could see was the word "Anywhere", the old man noticed that Thaddeus was gazing at the signs, "And that is your very destination my boy" he said chuckling, "I'm sorry?" asked Thaddeus slightly confused, he glanced down at Takt who looked just as confused. "Your destination, it can be anywhere…" replied the old man as he pointed a boney finger skywards towards the very top of his staff, "I know why the two of you have come my friends and I am here to send you on your way so to speak, my name is Manni Mais, I am the Man of the Corn" Manni said with an expecting look on his face, in truth the only one out of the pair who really knew who he was, was Takt who nodded at the man, but Thaddeus just looked at Manni Mais with a slightly sheepish smile across his face, but Manni was a friendly man and continued "I am the

Gatekeeper of sorts, I help those who wish to travel to the locations they desire, I have lived since the world began and it is my job now, to send you to your first destination" he said as he pointed a finger at the satchel around Thaddeus' shoulder, "In truth my boys, I already know where you need to go in order to find your first piece of the Todesfall Clock" with that Thaddeus and Takt looked surprised, the words of amazement could not escape Thaddeus' mouth and instead he just groaned and stared, Takt however managed a word or two, "How do you know all of this Manni?" he asked. "I know all my friend, I know everything about everything and more" he said, his voice was warm and friendly, it broke every now and again with different words and his accent was very strange, it sounded a mixture of a million different countries and more, but it suited him and Thaddeus liked that. "But there isn't much time to dilly dally so come with me" said Manni Mais and with that he turned and crookedly walked back through the corn stems. Thaddeus and Takt hurried after him and were soon walking close behind the old man not wanting to lose him in the maze of corn, the little old man soon stopped in what seemed to be a small clearing, still close with corn but there seemed to be more room to maneuver. The ground opened up slightly in front of them with what seemed to be broken corn stems strewn across the ground and then Thaddeus saw the Sidhee again, their colorful wings fluttered amongst the corn as they lowered. The man of the corn looked on without saying a word, he just closed his eyes, pointed a familiar finger and hummed an unusual hum, it sounded like the rumble of a waterfall but much quieter, it could be felt more than heard, felt deep within the heart of Thaddeus, with that Thaddeus looked down at Takt who had his zipper mouth agape, his pocket watch eyes staring forward in anticipation, Thaddeus placed a hand on his shoulder and they both looked on.

The humming of Manni Mais floated forward, the tall pieces of corn swayed as it passed by them until it reached the Sidhee who responded straight away, they fluttered over the broken pieces of corn which started to twitch and move as the snail fairies flew over them. Some of the fairies landed on the corn and shone brighter than the rest but soon all of the Sidhee seemed to shine a little brighter like small stars and with that not just the broken corn started to move. The corn that stood around the Sidhee started to bend, the broken pieces lifted from the floor and now stood straight, the broken pieces entwined the unbroken pieces of corn which bent and twisted with the movement, more corn crept out of the dirt and more twisted out of the surrounding corn field. The pieces wrapped and bent with audible creaks and cracks until they started to resemble a gate, or even a door. The corn wrapped tightly together until they formed a solid gate-like door, five large corn stems wrapped above the door to create an ornate archway, a handle emerged and was made of small beautiful blue flowers that had magicked themselves out of nowhere. With that the doorway was complete and Manni Mais stepped forward, "The quest you are embarking on is dangerous and you should take great care as I cannot go with you" stated the old man, the smile had now gone and was replaced now with a sterner look. Thaddeus and Takt nodded as the both stepped forward, listening to the old man "Keep your wits about you my friends and on your return I will be waiting to greet you" Manni said as he reached forward and opened the door, it creaked open with the very sound that Thaddeus had imagined, it creaked like bending corn but seemed so much more sturdier, through the doorway more corn could be seen standing tall and straight, it seemed to be the same field but something was different, it seemed darker through the doorway but Thaddeus stepped through without hesitation, a hand could be felt on his shoulder as he passed through, it reassured him and filled him with confidence that he had lacked for so long. Behind him he could hear metallic

footsteps and knew that Takt was close
behind.

"Your destination is the Maug Lake, it is
situated at the very centre of Fangenhex
Forest, north of the corn field, there is
great evil there so beware and keep one
another safe" said Manni Mais and with
that he shut the corn door and all was
quiet. The pair looked at each other, "Are
you ready?" asked Thaddeus, "As I will
ever be" responded Takt with a smile on
his face as the pair turned and started to
walk through the corn field, moving tall
pieces of the stiff corn from their path,
an audible creak could be heard and as
they turned they saw the corn door
collapsing into the ground, Manni Mais was
now truly gone.

They walked for what seemed like a long
time before they reached the edge of the
field, they stepped onto an old and
seemingly unused road, they crossed it and
followed a line of trees on their left and
the tall corn could still be seen for
miles to their right as they walked. The
sun was absent here and instead was
replaced by dark clouds that threatened
rain at any moment. They rounded a long
corner and then, to their left there was a
break in the trees and a trail that led
deep into a dark and damp looking forest.
Thaddeus drew from his satchel the papers
that Gideon Lilleyman had sketched,

scribbled and noted on many years ago, he looked at them and saw a small sketch of a trail leading into a forest, Thaddeus looked up and realized the path ahead bared the same resemblance as the drawing "This must be the place" called Thaddeus to Takt who was standing a few feet ahead looking into the forest. "There is evil in this forest, I can feel it" said Takt with a slight quiver in his voice, "So can I" replied Thaddeus as he stood alongside Takt. The pair looked ahead for a moment, what would they face in this dark place? What would be lurking within the Maug Lake? And would they ever see the sunlight again? Thaddeus pulled his collar tightly around his neck at the feel of the chilled air and looked at Takt who had done the same, his clockwork face bearing a stern look but as Takt looked up at Thaddeus he gave a look of reassurance and at that moment Thaddeus was glad he had Takt with him. The pair started out along the trail and towards whatever faced them in the forest.

8.

The Maug Lake.

Thaddeus and Takt had been walking for what seemed like hours, it was in fact only about one hour that they had been traversing the bumpy and tree laden forest. The floor had become increasingly harder to walk on as the pair frequently sunk knee deep into the oozing bog around them, it was sodden and had large twisted roots protruding from it with the mud now becoming thick with pools of deep black water forming in every step. Trees that sprouted from the mud had black bark with no leaves but still managed to stop the light from penetrating the canopy above, branches twisted and curled around the pair with which Thaddeus frequently banged his head on. The air was thick but cool with a mist that clung low to the ground and every now and again Thaddeus stopped and listened as there seemed to be a bubbling sound that echoed through the forest around them.

It wasn't much longer before the ground started to feel more solid under foot, the forest floor seemed to be rising slightly as the old crooked trees seemed to look a little more tree-like, the bark now

looking greener with small leaves now
being seen on some of the thin branches
that sprouted from the more ancient
looking branches. Thin spears of grass
sprung out at the bases of some of the
trees which seemed to have a faint shine
to them as tiny rays of light pierced the
overhead tree tops and seemed to shoot
straight into the dark floor, this gave
Thaddeus a small feeling of happiness in
this dark place. Thaddeus and Takt
Zifferblatt stopped for a short time at
the base of a great old tree, its bark was
dark grey and its roots were thick as they
sunk into the ground around them, the
branches were as thick as Thaddeus and
Takt put together but there was something
eerie about their choice of rest area as
no birds could be heard as Thaddeus eat a
bag of salt and vinegar crisps and a bacon
sandwich. Takt didn't need to eat as he
didn't technically have a human body and
wasn't technically alive. The sound of the
forest around them was quiet and still and
there wasn't a creak of a tree or a chirp
of bird, the earth lay still around their
feet and the tree they leant against felt
as though it was somehow watching them.

"Where do you suppose the person we are
meant to find is?" asked Thaddeus as he
looked over at Takt, "I am not sure" said
Takt as he pulled out the maps and papers
and glanced at them before replying "The
map says nothing of where to go once we

enter the forest, it does not even say a remote location within the forest where we could find the clock piece, but I have a strange feeling, I do not know if you feel it also, but it seems to be pulling me further into the forest, it could be an internal feeling or sense that is guiding us" Takt said and Thaddeus nodded in agreement "It could either be that, or it could be my nose pulling me towards that foul smell" Thaddeus said as he scrunched up his face, it was true in fact as in the last half an hour or so there had been a strange smell that seemed to be getting stronger the further they entered the forest. Takt Zifferblatt laughed, his zipper mouth falling open as he clapped his clockwork hands onto his clockwork knees, Thaddeus laughed as well before finishing his sandwich. He then packed the maps back into his satchel and stood, Takt stood as well and they both gazed up the hill behind the large tree. The top could be seen and they knew that was the way to go, they continued up the hill that now held large stones that were partially covered in moss, they clambered past with renewed energy and finally reached the top, how big was this forest? And where in the country were they? When Thaddeus had looked at the map earlier on in the day, the forest had been marked somewhere in the north of Scotland, and then Thaddeus realized that the corn field doorway had transported them from just outside of

Bristol all the way to north of Scotland in the blink of an eye, he chuckled slightly to himself in amazement before looking down at where they needed to walk next.

The hill angled down quite steeply and seemed nearly exactly the same as where they had just travelled from, the hill traveled down past large curled trees with nearly no leaves and in the distance the dark bowels of the forest could be seen, but then all around this area the hill in which they were stood on circled it. It looked like a giant crater where a forest had grown upon, the place they must reach seemed to be in the center of where they were facing but it wasn't clear how long it would take to get there. The pair started down the hill as they minded each step with caution, the ground was uneven as the moss made the ground spongy, trees acted as supports as they both held on to them to stop from sliding down the moss covered hill.

It didn't seem to take long before they reached the bottom, the air becoming moist and thick again as they tried to catch their breath from the previous descent. They moved as quickly as possible through the dank and dark forest, the water logged ground soaking over the feet of the travelers, "Do you think it's much further?" asked Thaddeus with strained

words as he fought against the bog that
surrounded them, "I hope not my friend, as
this forest is starting to get slightly on
my nerves, the ground is treacherous and I
always feel I will be dragged down into
the depths" Takt chuckled, Thaddeus
slipped into the mud up to his knees,
water dripped from the branches above with
smaller branches curling around the pair,
half submerged in the thick and foul muddy
forest ground. The moss was no longer
green and was now a dark brown, the mud
and thick misted air stained the fungus,
Thaddeus pulled himself out of the mud and
reached back for Takt's hand, pulling him
free of the bog.

The air smelt foul and seemed to be oozing
into Thaddeus' very skin, his hair was
stuck to his face with sweat and moisture
as he looked back at Takt he saw that the
fabric and shoe laces that were wrapped
tightly around him were a darker color
that before, dark with the damp that stuck
to their bodies and Takt's pocket watch
eyes had a thick layer of condensation on
them, the light green color that emitted
from the more human looking watch eyes
could still be seen glowing through the
moisture as he struggled through the
forest.

Suddenly, the ground went firmer and was
much easier to walk upon, "Finally" said
Takt "A little relief from the never

ending swamp" he continued as he wiped his metal hands over his fabric body, cleaning away the muck and dirt, "I thought we would be in that forever, that is my idea of hell I think, walking through that swamp for an eternity is definitely not for me" Thaddeus replied as they both laughed together. As they turned they saw that a slight trail was etched into the forest ground, petals of flowers and old tree leaves were strewn down the faint path and the trees seemed less foreboding, they glanced at each other and eagerly walked on, Thaddeus's legs ached and his back was sore from walking but his eagerness kept him going, he could rest when they reached the end of the trail, it didn't seem long before a slight opening in the trees ahead caught Thaddeus and Takt's attention. They kept moving not saying a word and before long the trail ended, blocked by a broken old fence that ran to the left and right of them, the small wooden pickets were moldy and cracked and from a distance you would not be able to tell there was even a fence present. The light that had been flowing over them as they walked the path a few moments ago had suddenly disappeared as they both looked ahead and past the fence with worried expressions. "It is the Maug Lake" said Takt still looking ahead, Thaddeus knew the name, not only from the map he possessed but also from what the Man of the Corn had said, "Your destination is the Maug Lake, it is situated at the very centre of Fangenhex Forest, north of the corn field, there is great evil there so beware and keep one another safe", the words echoed in Thaddeus' mind as a chill ran down his spine, the vision that was in front of him was enough to make anyone turn and run in the opposite direction, in the past that is exactly what he would of done, but not now, he wanted to see Pandora again and how would he feel if he ran from the very adventure that would allow him to see her face again and even talk to her. This thought spurred him on and without even saying a word to Takt he walked down a short length of the fence, Takt hurried after him until they both found a broken old gate that hung onto the fence at each side so very fragile looking. Thaddeus pushed the latch and opened the fence, it swung open silently and they passed through. Fog seemed to envelop them as they progressed forward as they seemed to step onto a stone path, the stones being large but uneven and had dark water on each side, small roots and twigs could be seen spearing out of the water's surface but not a ripple could be seen a sound be heard.

The mist curled around them but no win could be felt and as Thaddeus looked back at his companion all he could see was a faint silhouette and two glowing green eyes, "How are you doing back there Takt?" asked Thaddeus as his voice swept through the thick air, "I am fine, there is evil here, I can sense it, the air seems different and I can feel something drawing closer" replied Takt as he caught up slightly to Thaddeus, and in a matter of fact Thaddeus could feel it also as the air seemed full of something, something malevolent.

The visibility around them was poor and the mist covered most of the water that was to either side of them, in the distance out on the lake silhouettes could be seen of broken old trees with the old branches peering out of the stale smelling fog like black fingers. Ahead the outlines of a small bridge could be seen and as the pair approached they saw it was made from large crooked stones, it arched upwards a short way and then sloped downwards again, it wasn't clear what the bridge crossed but as Thaddeus and Takt crossed it a small rumbling or even growling could be heard coming from beneath that seemed to shake the stones the travelers stood upon.

They moved quickly on and hurried down the stone path as the fog seemed to ease slightly and as they continued they found themselves walking up a slight incline. The silhouette ahead seemed like a small mound with a great tree on top, its vast branches spread out with a brighter light behind it and this made the shadow that was painted onto the sky even more impressive, but something was different and Thaddeus wasn't sure what but it seemed like it was moving and then he realized something, the tree wasn't on top of the mound of earth but was behind it, Thaddeus' curiosity spurred him on, the ache and pains in his body subsided as he scrambled to the top of the mound. He needed to see this as his mind was telling him this was the destination, this was the first meeting and with Takt following hurriedly behind him they reached the top and peered down to the sight beyond.

9.

Bolgreena Mollhog.

The mound sank down into murky water, the
same water that they had just walked over
and as Thaddeus looked around he realized
that it was still part of the same lake,
the water ran around the mound which was
some form of island, the lake here had
much more debris with logs and branches
protruding the water like long, stiff
tarantula legs which lay perfectly still
until Thaddeus noticed something, they
weren't laying perfectly still, they were
actually moving, twitching and writing in
the water and as Thaddeus followed the
crooked shapes along he saw they were
attached to some form of hand which looked
very distorted, with that Thaddeus and
Takt stumbled down the earthy mound to the
water's edge, the water smelt stagnant and
the mist had nearly all but disappeared.
Takt looked on to the tree like shape
ahead and noticed there were large stones
in the water that could act as stepping
stones, Takt took the first step, "Is it
safe?" asked Thaddeus looking on in
anticipation as Takt looked back at him,
his face was stern "There is only one way
to find out, the stones seem stable" he
said as he pressed his metal foot down

hard on the first and then the second stone, the water around the base didn't even let a small ripple out, the top of the stones seem to shine slightly in the misty light with a gleam of moss covering them which made them slightly slippery.

Large logs and branches were broken and stuck out of the water to either side of them, moss hung like thick cobwebs from pieces of the large spider like branches with small wisps of mist that hung closely to the logs. They continued across the stones and saw the tree ahead before Takt stopped still, "What's wrong?" asked Thaddeus stopping behind him, "It's the witch" said Takt with a sense of fear in the glowing eyes and before either of them could speak again evil words floated across the misted air towards them, "Come closer" it said, and without even thinking they both moved forward across the moss covered stones. They moved slowly before hearing a noise coming through the mist, it was a raspy breathing sound that filled the air with a putrid stench so much so that Thaddeus felt like he was about to retch. The air filled his nostrils and made his eyes fill with water but they moved closer still, Takt Zifferblatt kept a hand back seemingly holding Thaddeus back slightly in a warding gesture, they moved closer still until they were able to see the tree more clearly, or was it a tree? The branches moved and twisted from side to side but not how a tree would normally move; there was no wind so nothing in the air could move the branches. Curiosity took over Thaddeus and he urged a reluctant Takt to move closer and then the voice sounded again, "Closer, I said" the voice was creaky like wood bending and was drawn out and very eerie but before long the two travelers were upon the origin of the voice. The tree was alive, but not how you would describe an everyday tree in the local park, this tree was actually alive as it had a face even though the face was hideous in appearance, with cracks and splits and pieces of bark that hung from the long chin. Thaddeus noticed something, this being the large wooden looking face in front of them was actually that of a woman, her eyes gleamed in the misty light and her chin hung low and long. The pattern of bark could just be seen in the dim light with her hair seeming to be long tendrils of moss that hung by her face. Her face was as craggy and dank as the setting around them and her neck was long and very crooked which connected to bulbous looking shoulders. Twigs and branches sprouted out of her shoulders which also held two long and crooked arms that Thaddeus had thought were sunken logs, her hands were long and crooked and seemed like two giant wooden spiders with long nails which had now turned to bark, the hands rested on two large boulders that were covered in a bright green moss and which seemed to glow slightly.

Thaddeus looked back at the face of the wooden woman which he now realized was the witch that Takt had spoken of moments ago. He gazed up and was stunned to see the tree he had seen from over the mound was actually attached to her, it was part of her head and sat atop it like a large crooked crown, the branches spanning out vastly but seemed to move with ease as the witch moved her head to peer at her two new visitors, "You visit me Thaddeus Loveguard and Takt Zifferblatt, you wish to take a treasure of mine and keep it for your own, you wish to see the dead again, oh how charming" she spoke with an eerie giggle that rung out across the still lake, the only other sound was the slight bubbling coming from the water at the witch's waist, her body was half submerged within the Maug Lake and seemed dark with moisture and mould where she connected with the water. When she spoke, her mouth cracked open like a tear and revealed thin pointed teeth that were like pieces of broken bark but seemed very sharp and hideously discolored. She moved forward to look at them more clearly, "Answer me insects" she bellowed and her voice changed to that of a volcano of mud beginning to erupt but still seemed to only be confined to the mist.

"We wish that Witch" spoke Takt loudly, his voice confident and determined, "Give us what we need as I know you have already seen why we are here and don't waste our time" he bellowed at her. She chuckled and evil laugh and looked right at Takt, "You cannot just take from me you puny thing, I am more powerful than you could ever imagine, I am Bolgreena Mollhog, you should fear me!" she shouted as each word grew more louder than the last, Takt straightened and spoke, "I know who you are Bolgreena, I know all about you and personally I find your tale a sad one" he said. Bolgreena Mollhog glared at him and then at Thaddeus who felt his fear rise up inside, "So what of you Thaddeus? Are you here to insult me as well?" she asked, her voice seeming to lower in tone slightly, "No" Thaddeus spoke with a quiver in his voice, "I simply want to acquire the piece of the Todesfall Clock that we believe you have, please understand that I desperately want to see my wife again if only for a moment. I wish it more than anything and ever since Takt came into my life and told me about the clock that his clock master told him of, I decided I would stop at nothing to get it" Thaddeus spoke every word to the witch with great belief, he didn't care or really notice the expression the witch had across her hideous face, but he didn't care, he needed the clock piece and knew he would get it or die trying.

"So please, allow us the clock piece or allow us to do something that would make you trust us enough to give it to us, please Bolgreena, I know you are good, there must be good in you and I beg you to find it" he continued and with the words he didn't even notice Takt shoot him a concerned look as he thought of having to do something for the tree-like witch in front of them. Bolgreena Mollhog looked at the pair for a long moment, her large and dark eyes glistened from Thaddeus to Takt before her half submerged body tilted forward, the large tree atop her ragged head moved with her movements and then she craned her neck towards them. The creaking of her limbs moving filled the air around them, the branches that crowned her head creaked and cracked, rustling with the movements until her face was only a couple of feet from them, her breath smelt of stagnant water as she breathed out gently and her face could be better seen now and was bark like all over. Her skin didn't crease it just seemed to stay the same as she looked at them both in turn. She giggled again which sounded loud in their ears as she was much closer now, Thaddeus could feel drips on his face and hair and noticed large droplets of water were dripping from the branches above and from the witch's moss like hair. Insects crawled out of nostrils that were hidden under a large branch like nose; dead leaves were squashed into her bark skin and looked like black slime that glistened. She opened her mouth, a black hole in the tree face lined with the thin and yellow bark teeth and spoke, "There is something you can do for me" she said grinning at them.

Thaddeus and Takt looked at each other worriedly, but before they were able to utter a word Bolgreena hissed her demand, "I once had a necklace that was dear to me and it had a crest with a skull imbedded into it, the chain was golden and twisted like ivy with a golden clasp on it. It was sadly lost into the mud that bubbles around you, if you venture into the mud and retrieve it I will give you your precious piece of Todesfall Clock, so what say you?" she said in an almost whisper, her words like a harsh breeze around the travelers with her glaring eyes just feet from their faces. She was so close her long chin dipped slightly into the stagnant mud and her long teeth were at their eye level, her lips curled into a grotesque grin. Thaddeus didn't even consult Takt in his reply, he knew that Takt would agree with whatever he said, they were companions in the same quest and they would stay that way until the end, "We accept" Thaddeus said, loud, clear and straight into the face of the hideous and ancient tree witch. With that Bolgreena looked slightly shocked, but only slightly as it may have surprised her that they would agree. Thaddeus glanced to Takt after his response and saw that he was nodding with his clockwork face looking stern and confident. "Very well" the witch said, "Step into the mud in front of you".

Thaddeus took the first step, the mud ahead of him looked thick and black with large bubbles that would rise and then pop on the surface. He could feel Bolgreena's breath on the back of his neck as he looked down at the swampy liquid that surrounded the stone he and Takt stood upon, the stench of her breath was overpowering and he could feel her cold and eerie stare watching down in anticipation. Thaddeus was pretty sure that he may be stepping into a trap but he felt he had nothing to lose. He felt Takt Zifferblatt move behind him, the familiar metallic sound of his feet rang out in the misty silence that surrounded them as Thaddeus placed his worn footwear into the engulfing mud, it felt cool and thick around his ankle and then his leg was cool up to his knee and before he knew it he was waist deep in the slimy and stagnant bog, he could feel, something worm past his legs as he stood there and when he looked back at Takt he saw the clockwork man stepping next into the thick liquid. Thaddeus glanced up at the witch who seemed to be towering above them, her eyes staring and her mouth smiling creepily at them and Thaddeus noticed she looked so

much bigger from down in the muddy swamp,
her arms stretched out in front of them
but one hand was no longer placed on one
of the large moss-covered boulders that
still seemed to be glowing through the
grey air. The hand moved through the air
with a creak like that of a mighty oak
that swayed in the wind, but Thaddeus
thought that Bolgreena Mollhog was pretty
much a mighty oak and maybe in the next
few hundred years she may transform
completely into one and be unable to move
at all.

The hand came closer until it was hanging
right above Thaddeus and Takt, her eyes
gleamed through the fingers as they
twitched and bent above the travelers.
Then her mouth opened slightly as whispers
came tumbling from the hideous and rotten
maw, the language was something that
Thaddeus had never heard in all of his
little life, "It is the language of the
Dollgrat" said Takt quietly to Thaddeus in
order that the witch could not hear them,
"What is the Dollgrat?" asked Thaddeus
still not taking his eyes off of the
actions of the witch, the cold of the mud
that oozed around him started to make him
quiver and shake with constant chills as
he held the satchel above the mud so it
wouldn't get wet or damaged. "The Dollgrat
is an ancient language from long ago, if I
am not mistaken, those boulders she places
her hands upon are the Dollgrat stones,

stones that possess an immeasurable amount of magic, they were mostly believed to be myth and so was the tale of Bolgreena but apparently, they are real. If we make it out alive I will tell you the tale in more detail" Takt said as he also kept his large, glowing pocket watch eyes on the large witch, "You are correct Takt Zifferblatt, and I will wait with baited breath to see if you both return" Bolgreena said suddenly from above and with that the mud around Thaddeus and Takt seemed to loosen under foot, they felt themselves starting to slip further under the oozing liquid and before long they were neck deep. The bubbles bubbled around their faces as Takt grabbed for Thaddeus, Thaddeus found Takt's metal fingers with a clockwork and fabric wrist and he grabbed, he grabbed hard and didn't let go, the last thing they heard was the witch laughing loudly as they sank deeper. The stench of the mud was toxic and nauseating and then suddenly, the mud consumed the two of them.

Thaddeus felt the area around him shift, his grip still tightly holding Takt's hand, the mud was loosening and then tightening, it seemed to be turning and falling with large droplets of mud seemingly dripping within the mud as Thaddeus thought he felt himself sliding back upwards. Thaddeus opened his eyes under the mud and saw the thick brown,

green and black slime seeming to shift and
fall around him and then suddenly he felt
a tugging on his hand, Takt felt as if he
was hanging from Thaddeus' hand and then,
quicker than Thaddeus could think, he
fell. The mud fell in thick strands around
him like large spears seeming to fall from
the sky and Thaddeus felt himself fall
hard onto his back. The ground was solid
but with a slight wet and lumpy feel,
Thaddeus got a look upwards at where he
had fallen and it seemed like the sky
which was as low as a room ceiling was
actually, moving, moving like the muddy
swamp that they had stepped into just a
few moments ago. It slimed above him in
thick swirls and bubbled but the thick
black bubbles were upside down as they
popped and sprayed from the low sky above.
Thaddeus got to his feet and saw Takt
stood a few feet away and it was only then
that Thaddeus saw his surroundings; they
seemed to be stood on an old cobbled
street, a street that resembled
Giggleswick Street, but this wasn't
Gigglewick Street even though the cobbles
seemed familiar and the buildings looked
vaguely the same but this place was
deserted, the buildings were broken and
falling apart with thick slime from above
running down the brickwork and oozing down
the edges of the street. The bricks of the
buildings were black as night and so were
the windows, so much so that they could
not be seen through. Thaddeus and Takt

didn't like this new but familiar world, the air stank of a sickening odor that smelt a mixture of stagnant water and garbage bags that had been forgotten about, but Thaddeus knew they had a job to do and so did Takt and as they looked at each other they nodded before setting off down the rancid and oozing streets to find the witch's necklace.

They had been walking for only a short time, making sure they didn't slip on the slimy cobbled streets whilst Takt peered through some of the dirty windows. Not a soul was present in the creepy streets and in the air there was a strange sound, Thaddeus cocked his head to listen more whilst Takt continued to peer through each window, scraping the muck off of the crusted windows but to no avail as the inside of the buildings were dark and lifeless. Thaddeus listened more but could not identify the sound and could not locate where it was coming from, "Takt, can you hear that?" Thaddeus asked as Takt stopped for a moment, looked back at Thaddeus and listened to the air, "I can't hear anything" He replied and turned back to checking the windows and moving slowly down the crooked and bleak street. Thaddeus brushed it off for now and joined Takt, he tried locks on the doors which were locked tightly and as he glanced down the alleyways he saw shadows moving that may have only been his imagination. Thick black ooze slimed down from the center of an archway that the pair passed under and now the brick was unrecognizable, looking almost like a large open mouth that belonged to a hideous and slimy giant. Just as the travelers had dodged the thick blobs that fell around them, the sound that Thaddeus had heard a few minutes before sounded again, this time Takt heard it as well and he stopped in his tracks. Thaddeus stopped next to him as they both listened, they heard it ringing across the dark and damp land, this time louder than before and also much clearer before Thaddeus realized it was quite a pleasant tune, it sounded like chimes of small bells ringing musically but then Thaddeus realized what it was, it was a much louder version of a musical jewelry box.

Thaddeus and Takt moved in the direction they thought the sound was coming from but then something stopped Thaddeus again, "I feel like something is watching us" said Thaddeus as he glanced up and down the street, his eyes wandered up to the high windows that seemed to tower above them in the buildings that looked like they were once shops. He saw thick streams moving down the side of the buildings, but something seemed different as the streams seemed to move in different directions, they oozed right and then left, then back up the side of the building before rapidly falling back down towards Thaddeus and

Takt. As the ooze began to approach the slime started to build in volume, then Takt nudged Thaddeus and as he looked across he noticed that more slimy blobs were sliding down the adjacent buildings, their mucky trails oozed over the dirty windows and slid faster as they approached the ground, "We must get out of here" shouted Takt as he grabbed Thaddeus' arm and pulled, they fled down the cobbled streets now slipping every other step as the ground seemed to be more slippery than before, Thaddeus glanced back and all he saw were many different slimy blobs moving rapidly behind them. The thick black bodies oozed and writhed as they pursued the companions; thick tendrils splashed out and broke windows of the dilapidated buildings that edged the road Thaddeus and Takt were dangerously sprinting on. Takt had spotted a route for escape and pulled Thaddeus down an alleyway, it smelt badly down the narrow and crooked passageway Thaddeus thought to himself, it was like rotting meat and stagnant water. Takt looked for another route as they stood at a sudden dead end, then Thaddeus kicked at a door and it broke with unusual ease. They clambered inside and then all went quiet, not a sound was coming from outside where the oozing beasts had followed them and not a sound coming from within the building they stood in.

Thaddeus felt cold within this building, the walls were damp and the floor seemed molded as well as the air smelling musty and very old but then something caught Thaddeus' attention, it was the music they had heard before, the chiming tunes of the jewelry box this time however, it was coming from beneath them. Takt looked down and then back up at Thaddeus, "I think we should investigate" said Takt as he looked back down at the dusty ground again, "I agree" replied Thaddeus, "The sound seems louder here, maybe someone is living down there that knows the location of the necklace" continued Thaddeus as he walked towards the almost invisible staircase at the back of the room. The room they were in was almost pitch black accept for the dim light that came from the bleak outside world, it wasn't much but it provided enough light to navigate, Takt's eyes were useful as they came closer to the stairwell as they were able to shine a green light into the darkness. Tall empty shelving scattered the room, nothing was stored on them and they were covered in thick slimy ooze which was not much dissimilar from the ooze that covered the outside walls, Thaddeus took the first step down the stairs, there was no creak like he thought there might be and come to think of it there wasn't any sound in this world, everything seemed to absent of that kind of noise and instead just seemed to be decaying in the ooze that filled the

air and covered the land from above. Takt
followed quickly behind as they progressed
down the stairs but before long the light
had completely disappeared. Thaddeus drew
the small torch that was hidden in the
pouch which was fastened around his waist,
next to the screwdriver and small hammer.
He pressed the small rubber button and
suddenly light sprayed from the end of the
torch and cascaded down the empty
staircase. Before long Thaddeus and Takt
Zifferblatt had reached the bottom of the
stairs and were now standing at the end of
a long corridor, its walls seemed crooked
in the way that one wall was taller than
the other and gave the low ceiling a
slanted feel. They progressed and noticed
there was only one door at the end of the
corridor, light flickered from underneath
it which gave an eerie orange glow.
Thaddeus noticed that the light danced
every now and again as they approached, it
looked as if there was movement beyond the
black door but no sound apart from the
chiming music could be heard. The air was
heavy in the corridor and the walls were
damp but were absent of the slime like it
wasn't able to reach this low level just
yet. The light from the torch flickered as
Thaddeus's hand quivered but Takt noticed
this and placed a reassuring metal hand on
his forearm before smiling at him. The
music was louder now as they got ever so
close to the door, but now there was
another sound, it was like a winding of a

large toy which Thaddeus and Takt thought
to be strange as they frowned in confusion
at each other. They moved closer until
they were standing close to the door,
Thaddeus listened to the top portion of
the door and Takt leant down and listened
to the lower portion, both hearing the
same music and sound. Takt reached for the
black door handle, its ornate pattern now
faded with time and neglect and as Takt
twisted the handle the sound of winding
creaks stopped. Thaddeus held his breath
in fear and anticipation as Takt continued
to turn the handle, and with a force they
both pushed the door open quickly and were
shocked by what they found.

10.

A box of jewels and dolls.

The room before Thaddeus and Takt
glimmered an orange color as two gas lamps
that were sitting on small ornate tables
glowed brightly. Sitting around the walls
of the small room were dolls, so many
dolls that Thaddeus didn't have the time
to count them all, there were large ones
and small ones, ones that seemed to be
from a distant time that were worn and
fragile looking. Some were porcelain that
stared at Thaddeus and Takt with unmoving
eyes. It was eerie Thaddeus thought to
himself and he was quite sure that Takt
thought it as well because when he looked
down at his clockwork companion, he was
certain there was a grimacing look in his
clockwork face. Thaddeus felt a certain
feeling of unease in this small box shaped
room. On the walls hung some kinds of
paintings but the paintings were badly
faded and could not be identified as to
their content. Takt moved forward once he
had become accustomed to the sense in the
room and began to look around for possible
clues as to the Witch of the Maug's
necklace, there was nothing, not even
writings or drawings of anything, Thaddeus
felt frustrated and who knows how large

this world is and if it is incredibly large then how were they to find the necklace. Then Takt gasped slightly, "What's the matter?" asked Thaddeus, "I believe we are in the Malimar" stated Takt, a quiver in his voice as he held a rectangular box with intricate carvings all over, and Thaddeus realized the box look similar to the chest they had acquired Gideon Lilleyman's life research from.

This chest that Takt held looked different however and Thaddeus felt as though this very chest in the hands of his friend was evil, "What is the Malimar" asked Thaddeus still not taking his eyes off of the chest, its carvings were incredibly detailed and its lock was a dim golden color, it had red stains that were imbedded into the design and Thaddeus could have been certain that the stains were blood. The box had large hinges that looked like claws which protruded from the back of the box furthest from Takt's metal fingers, "The Malimar is an evil place, it is a place of death and decay and where foul creatures lurk and feed the rotting stench into the human's world, remember the Domovoy?" asked Takt as Thaddeus nodded, remembering the hairy and evil man that laughed and pointed at the two of them in the train station, he hoped it wasn't lurking down here in the Malimar, "Well the Domovoy can see in to the

Malimar and can see into Earths world, he
can communicate with the dark creatures
and can walk amongst humans which makes
him extremely dangerous. The way I know we
are in the Malimar is firstly from the
oozing monsters that chased us and also
from the carvings that embed this chest I
hold" Thaddeus looked more closely at the
chest and saw that it looked like a dried
version of the ooze which covered the
walls, it was lumpy and rigid, with blobs
extending from each corner and strands
that looked like tendrils wrapped in coils
all over the lip of the box. With this
knowledge Thaddeus did not want Takt to
open the chest but he knew he would have
to see what was inside. The chest lid
creaked as Takt Zifferblatt prized the
thick object apart and peered his large
eyes into the small area of darkness.
Thaddeus moved to stand behind Takt and
looked over his small, woven shoulders;
the darkness edged away as the golden
light that surrounded them and the doll
crept into the box and then, stood before
them on a small black platform and in
front of a small oval mirror was a thin
ballet dancer. Her arms were arched above
her head and her legs twined together like
ivy. She was perched on tip toes in small
red ballet shoes with her dress looking
worn from years of neglect and her black
hair now chipped away to reveal white
paint underneath. The oval mirror behind
was smeared with dust and dirt with the

lining and inside of the box being caked
in a thick grey dust.

The music that Thaddeus expected to hear
from the music box was absent but then,
just as Thaddeus thought this, the small
dancer twitched and jerked around in a
creaky twirl and the music that was
expected sounded loudly from the box. But
as it sounded the light in the room
flickered, it flickered in time with the
music and then as the music stopped with a
sudden halt the light went out, if only
for a moment but it was a moment that
seemed to last forever with only the sound
of Thaddeus' breathing filling the small
room. Then the room flickered with the
golden light again, Thaddeus could see a
shadow moving, then another, and then
another as three shadows moved from the
piles of dolls that surrounded them with
each flicker of golden lamp light. The
movements were jerky and much like a doll
but Thaddeus couldn't see the full detail
of the unknown figures but could only see
the limp limbs hanging by their sides.
They seemed to be wearing dresses and as
they moved steadily closer Thaddeus and
Takt moved backwards as with each edgy
step the two companions had increasing
senses of fear but as Takt looked back at
the door he noticed it had been shut. One
of the shadowy figures was stepping in
front of their only exit; they stood
closely together as the dark strangers

stepped together with one stood in front of the other two. The light seemed to be getting more erratic but as it started to settle it fell on the faces of the trio and Thaddeus and Takt saw them for what they were. The faces of the three were hidden behind white masks which were slightly cracked at the edges and seemed to be made from porcelain just like some of the dolls that littered the edges of the room around them. Two black holes in the masks where eyes should be stared at Thaddeus and Takt Zifferblatt lifelessly and a small slit where the mouth should have been was unmoving and gave no indication of what hid behind the eerie masks. The figures wore dresses much like ballet dancers and stepped closer in the form of a dancer but much more animated, like wind up dolls and as the trio approached slowly a strange winding noise could be heard as the joints ticked and clicked with each movement. The posture of them did not change and neither did the position of the two mannequin like figures that followed behind the seeming leader of the creepy group. Thaddeus felt strange as he stared at them and felt as though he couldn't move but the funny thing was that he didn't really want to move, he felt very at ease and peaceful as the doll like creatures moved towards him every few minutes but this strange hypnotism like spell did not work on Takt. The clockwork man looked round at the dolls that lay propped up against the walls of the room, he noticed that they didn't all look like dolls and some looked as if they were wearing strange, painted and doll like masks, he realized something and that something was that they weren't dolls but people, or creatures that had come to this land or maybe they had been sent or lured here by the evil cries of Bolgreena Mollhog. Takt didn't have much time to think on this and as he looked up at the three demon dolls he saw that the leader, the one with scraggy blonde hair that didn't look entirely real was wearing a golden necklace around her thin and crooked neck, on it hung a skull just like the witch described and the chain was thick and twisted. Takt moved quickly towards the dolls and Thaddeus, he could feel an energy inside of himself, an energy that burnt and felt as if it was glowing but when Takt glanced down at himself he saw that he was actually glowing, well his long hands were, his ornate fingers shined with a blue light that seemed serene but also ghostly and at that moment he remembered a spirit he had encountered not much time after he had died. The spirit was a tall man with a top hat and tails, his hair was long and thin just like the rest of his body but he had strange glowing white eyes, the man had told him some of the ways of being a ghost, ways that had helped Takt Zifferblatt greatly in his ghostly years.

There was a type of power that ghosts
possessed which helped them in fighting
demons and it would show itself when the
ghost needed it the most. The power was
called the StarkStrom and was a spirits
greatest weapon next to knowledge, but as
Takt looked down at his glowing hands it
seemed as if time had slowed dramatically,
he looked up at the demons in front of
him, the Jewel Box Dolls. He heard the
chiming music from the evil box sounding
slower than normal, he ran at the dolls
and raised his glowing clockwork hands as
bright light shone from them and fired a
beam of electric straight at the leader of
the dolls, the beam lit up the room
instantly and broke Thaddeus' trance.
Thaddeus blinked then dived to the floor
as Takt shouted "Get down!!" to him, the
beam sounded a powerful sound that seemed
to crack through the room. The leader of
the room's evil occupants slid back as it
raised a hand to shield itself. The other
two scattered but still adopted rigid
movements and fell to the dark shadows of
the room as the leader stood and stared at
Takt before raising its hands in a
pirouette motion before starting to twirl
on the spot. The chiming music rang out
louder than before as Thaddeus crawled to
Takt and grabbed at his metal hand which
helped him to his feet. Thaddeus pulled
the only weapon he had which was his
trusted screwdriver, its dark red handle
clutched tightly in his hand and the long

metal rod with a pointed Phillips head extended outwards in a defending motion. The companions held tightly onto each other as the light from Takt's hands subsided to a faint glow that outlined the clock hand fingers, but every now and again the fingers emitted small sparks that shot out in different directions. "Whats happening?" shouted Thaddeus over the not only clinking and chiming music but now there was a hissing screech that was coming from the wind-up demon's hidden mouth "They are some form of demon, the dolls that surround us are dead things, humans and other creatures that have fallen to the Jewel Box Dolls, they dwell in this room and take parts from the creatures they kill before turning them into dolls for eternity" shouted Takt back at Thaddeus, "Why are your hands glowing? asked Thaddeus as he glanced quickly at Takt's blue hands before looking back at the masked evil in front of them, his screwdriver raised toward it "It's the StarkStrom, a form of ghost magic, I didn't realize I possessed it as it only shows itself in time of need, and I guess this is a—" said Takt before stopping. The once still dead things at the sides of the rooms began to move, the arms and legs of them twitched before some started to sit up straight. Thaddeus stared with wide-eyed horror as he saw the crudely stitched limbs and crookedly cracked masks starting to move in formation to surround the

trapped duo. Joining them were the other
Jewel Box Dolls and Thaddeus hurriedly
looked away to avoid their hypnotic stare.
"Takt?" shouted Thaddeus, "Use the power
you have, it's the only way, kill them
all!!" he continued to shout and without
hesitation Takt's hands glowed brightly
and not only his hands but the area around
where his heart would be but now sat a
large silver clock cog glowed bright blue.
Electric looking sparks spat at the air
that surrounded them as he raised his
hands and blasted the room with electric
light. The hands of the dead dolls which
were just about to grab them both out of
the gloom but suddenly recoiled. The light
and sparks blasted into the broken bodies,
it swirled in the air and crashed into the
cracked walls, the pictures that hung
there smashed with audible cracking and
breaking sounds, glass shattered on the
ground and the now dead enemies were
forced back, their bodies crumpling onto
the ground as their masks smashed apart.

Two of the evil dolls were sent flying
across the room but no sooner had they hit
the ground did they tick and tock back to
standing positions. The light from Takt
surrounded them both, "Thaddeus, the
leader, you must kill the leader!" Takt
shouted, "But how? Nothing hurts them!"
Replied Thaddeus, fear was absent from his
voice and was now replaced with an anger,
but more so a determination to defeat

these monsters as he now saw the golden necklace that hung around the evil demon's neck, "Your screwdriver, you must pierce it into the heart, it is made of clockwork like mine, you must jam the clockwork!" and with that Thaddeus locked the masked monster in his sights, it was no longer hissing and summoning it's minions but was now looking right at them with its hand raised, pointing at them, it twitched in place as its head cocked to one side. Thaddeus looked from side to side and saw some of the dead things that were no longer incapacitated edging towards them, their masks cracked to reveal hideous, faceless monsters who had no eyes or mouths but instead large scars and a thin, creasing mouth that opened to reveal rotten and broken teeth, some had once been human but were no longer the way they had been. He looked ahead as Takt's blue StarkStrom shone around him, the sparks and bolts spinning around Thaddeus as he started to run forward, his screwdriver posed in a stabbing position. He ran with his eyes locked downwards, the room now seemed larger; the walls had broken away and seemed to make the room longer. Thaddeus ran but it felt to him as though long moments passed as he stepped one foot in front of the other before— He leapt, he leapt as high as he could, the blue light hitting away the outstretched arms that reached to stop Thaddeus, the crooked, thin and wretched hands blinded from touch

for a moment, and in that moment Thaddeus
struck with force and felt the screwdriver
pierce through skin that was no longer
skin but was more prosthetic feeling, and
then he felt metal grinding against metal
as he put all his weight against the demon
doll and twisted against the cogs within
it. He looked up at the masked face as he
felt the gears grind to a halt, the mask
hid the face behind even from this close
but Thaddeus could smell the old, rotten
decay of the dead things it had used to
live on for eternity. It grinded and
creaked, the limbs fell limp and the head
started to sag and in its final moments it
jerked and began to fall apart in
Thaddeus' hands, pieces of gears and cogs
crumbled in his grasp until they lay in a
pile on the floor. The masked head lay a
top the pile with items of the torn
clothing scattered around Thaddeus's feet.
Thaddeus breathed heavily as the
adrenaline subsided, he didn't even notice
Takt's blue lightening start to fade and
then finally disappear, he finally looked
up at Takt and noticed all of the beings
that were about to take hold of them and
turn them into dead dolls were all— dead,
they lay lifeless on the floor, broken and
unmoving and so were the two masked demons
that followed the evil wind-up ballet
doll. They lay in pieces on the floor on
either side of Takt, the walls were
scorched and smoldering around them with
large cracks now formed. Takt walked over,

leaned down and picked the spotless and golden necklace from the pieces of metal on the ground, Thaddeus stared down at it with thoughts racing through his mind, his life had changed drastically in the last few weeks and with what he knew now, his life would never be the same again and a more pressing thought ran through his head, what would be in store for them in the next coming weeks, or months, or even years? But Takt was standing in front of him now giving him a wide smile through the zipper lips that were stitched onto the fabric face. Thaddeus noticed that he seemed a little more human every time he took the time to properly look at his now haunted creation. "We did it Thaddeus" said Takt still smiling, "You did amazingly" he continued as Thaddeus smiled back at him, "So did you, I couldn't have done it without you" said Thaddeus, "We make a great team" said Takt who began to walk towards the now broken door, "Together I know we will be able to defeat anything" he said as he looked back at him, Thaddeus knew he was right, when he was with Takt he felt safe, like he was a guardian for him and little did he know that Takt thought exactly the same thing. They were fast becoming the best of friends which drove the pair to look out for one another just like the Man of the Corn had said before they set out to find the Witch in the Maug swamp.

They both walked back up the stairs that they had traveled down wearily almost an hour before, not knowing what they were about to face and as they reached the door that led out into the ooze filled streets they felt an ease of relief, even the black sludge that gathered in nearly every corner of the streets and which ran down the walls into the blocked gutters and drains felt much better to the hellish ordeal they had just endured, but something looked different about the street outside of the alleyway that they stood within, they ran forward now weary from the fight and were soon stood within the street where they saw something very peculiar. In front of them was a large black stream of a mud like substance, it fell from the oozing sky above but when it touched the slimy cobbled streets the ooze did not run anywhere, it stayed just oozing and swirling around like it was standing before them, but then something moved within the mud. A long crooked arm reached out of the thick slime followed by a long thin leg that was robed in a ragged looking dress which seemed to be made from cobwebs and leaves, Thaddeus looked up and saw two large eyes beginning to emerge from the slime as well as long, matted hair that curtained a hideous face, a face that seemed to be crusted with bark and dead leaves. The form began to emerge fully and Thaddeus realized just before Takt that it was Bolgreena Mollhog but in

a more human shape, she was no longer half
submerged in the thick swamp but now had
legs and a regular sized body. Her head
finally slipped through the mud and
revealed the tree a top her head but now
it was smaller, still looking like a
twisted and horned crown as it moved with
her twisted head movements as she inched
fully out from the tunnel of slime that
enveloped her and began to walk over to
the companions. Her hands creased in front
of her as if she was warding them away,
she was bent over and crooked looking and
her skin shone dully in the dim light with
the bark that covered her skin glistening
with the wet mud that caked her. She
walked right up to Takt and peered at the
necklace in his hand, reaching a long and
twig like hand forward she took the
necklace in her gnarled hand and began to
fasten it around her neck, not saying
anything at all she stared at them before
a child like smile creased her monstrous
face as she suddenly spoke to them, "You
did well, for insects" she hissed and
before she could speak again Thaddeus
interrupted "How are you this size and
form? And not, you know?" he gestured with
his arms in a manner that implied the size
they had previously seen her as, Bolgreena
swung her head towards him, her bare foot
stepping closer on the greasy cobbled
street with a wet slap, Thaddeus was
unaware of anything around him, not the
tall and crooked black buildings that

stood high to either side of the three of them, or of the slime that dripped from the sky and onto his shoulder, Bolgreena noticed though and with a long bent finger she dipped it into the ooze that sat on Thaddeus' shoulder, reached to her thin lips and tasted it, "Mmmm" she said closing her large eyes, "I forgot the taste of decay" she continued as she peered down at Thaddeus and Takt through dark eyes.

"I am this form because I wish it, the Dollgrat stones allow me to do many different things and one of them being the ability to transport myself to different places, including the Malimar" she said gesturing with her arms to the land around them, "Although I still have to reside within the Maug Lake, I can take my mind on journeys to different lands and appear as the beautiful woman you see before you" she gestured to herself as Thaddeus and Takt looked on but both thinking how warped a view the Witch had of beauty "I am more powerful than you both could ever possibly imagine, but I am of my word and you did retrieve this precious relic for me, so I will pay you for your troubles" and with that the hideous Witch reached into her near see-through robes that allowed Thaddeus and Takt to see her form underneath which looked a deep green color. The Witch took out two small packages, both wrapped in the skin of some form of dead animal, the fur was black and grey but that was all Thaddeus could determine as he took one package and Takt the other. Thaddeus quickly opened his and found not a piece of clock like he had hoped, but instead a pair of large goggle-like glasses that had large black lenses, the arms to them were long and dark grey with an intricate design carved into them of ivy and some form of tentacle pattern. The lenses held golden, crooked spirals that circled around the wearer's eyes when they wore the glasses. Thaddeus looked up in bemusement at the Witch as she smiled at him, "The glasses you hold in your hands are called the Glasses of Obsidian, they allow you to see your goals and also allow you to see magic both light and dark, just remember "Black as Black to see so clear" she said with her hand raised as if a teacher would when posing a question to the class and with that she turned to Takt Zifferblatt, who was opening his animal skin package carefully, within it sat a large metallic cog, it looked just like the piece that sat in Takt's chest, it shone in the dim light and had several smaller red cogs attached to it, a piece of dark blue casing held the fragmented clock pieces together and in the center of the large cog sat what seemed to be a quarter of a green sapphire, its jagged edge made Thaddeus think it had been broken at one time, "You know what that is" the Witch said not looking at either of them but instead stared straight at the clock piece, gleaming at the sight of it, seeing the Witch's gaze Takt covered it with the animal skin and put it in Thaddeus's satchel along with the Obsidian Glasses. "You need two more pieces" she said raising her two long and crooked twig fingers, "I am sure you are both clever enough to locate them but in case your small brains cannot think of where to travel next, maybe you should go to the Dandelion Fields, just north of FlugelBlume Forest, you will find what you are looking for there" she said, "Now close your eyes, and hold the breath in your lungs" and with that they both did as she asked.

A warm sensation fell upon them and then light seemed to shine on the outside of Thaddeus' closed eyes, Takt held his long hands over the pocket watch eyes he had as he didn't have eyelids but he felt the same sensation as Thaddeus, they felt as if they were floating for a moment but then a great weight fell upon their shoulders as they fell a short distance into a large grassy field. Thaddeus looked around as he opened his eyes, they were out of the Malimar and back in his world, sat in a large field that stretched and rolled away for miles, small white flowers dotted the grassland with the bluest sky Thaddeus had ever seen hung above them like the ocean. Takt was next to Thaddeus equally amazed at the sight that surrounded them; they stood and looked around some more before deciding to eat something as it felt as if they had gone without food for years.

It didn't take long for Thaddeus to eat his tin of tuna and drink the tiny bottle of water that was now warm from being concealed in his satchel for so long, Thaddeus remembered that Takt didn't eat anything as he saw his clockwork friend wander around the surrounding land to get his bearings as Thaddeus finished his food.

Before long they were ready to move and decided to head north as that was the direction the FlugelBlume Forest was in, it was on the map at least and they thought that Bolgreena must have had the decency to drop them at a decent enough distance away. They walked for a long time but enjoyed the bright sunlight as it was a welcome sight from the dim, dreary and slime filled land they had just been within. They were now ready for the next part of their journey and had no idea what may be in store for them.

11.

The Dandelion House.

Thaddeus and Takt walked for many hours through the field of green and white, all the while the sun shone brightly in the blue sky above and they were pleased to have a change of scenery, although the stench of the Malimar still clung to their clothes like a parasite and served as a constant reminder of the ordeal they had just survived. "So what is the story with Bolgreena?" asked Thaddeus as they walked, "She used to look human, but her appearance is all due to magic, her need for power and her fear of losing it" replied Takt as they came to a halt. They then sat on the grass for a well deserved rest before Takt continued "She is ancient, nobody knows how old exactly but she has been on this Earth for thousands of years at least, she practiced magic for most of her human life and when she learnt of two stones that could supply her with unlimited power, she quickly left in search for the relics known as the Dollgrat Stones" said Takt, "The stones were found in the Maug Lake which we know all too well and once you have placed your hands upon them, you are bound to them forever and would share in the power they

possess, the only trouble was when
Bolgreena placed her hands on the magical
objects she became trapped in the lake,
but she also feared that she may lose the
power if she separated herself from them
and in the end the power consumed her as
she was slowly transformed into the
monster you saw in the lake. Her power is
great but her soul has changed as she no
longer sees the good in the world and only
cares for herself, the power changed her
physically as her blood became mud and her
skin bark, her hair became moss and she
grew in size to hold the power she
received but one day she will cease to
exist and the magic will win, turning her
completely into the earth magic she is
feeding off" and with that Thaddeus
thought strongly about Bolreena, was it
her fault she was the way she was now? Or
did she deserve the fate she would one day
receive? Because when Takt gave her the
necklace in exchange for the piece of
clock, Thaddeus saw something in those
dark eyes even though he couldn't quite
identify it but there was something that
flickered there, this gave Thaddeus hope,
hope that her soul wasn't covered entirely
in the mud that surrounded her.

They walked on and it couldn't have been
more than thirty minutes later that they
topped a small green hill and gazed down
on a beautiful site, there in the valley
that was surrounded by small rolling green

hills just like the one they stood on, were curled trees with all different colored leaves and twisted branches that seemed old but in a more inviting way, more welcoming than the trees they had seen on their journey so far. The air seemed to be slightly misted against the blue sky and swirled with the slight breeze, at the foot of the trees that scattered the green valley was a thin layer of mist which hung close to the trunks as if protecting them. Along the ground were small pink, blue, purple and red flowers and there were also small white flowers that when looked at in more detail turned out to be dandelions, dandelions that were having small white seeds escaping the round heads in the breeze that flowed freely through the valley. Thaddeus realized that the mist that was floating into the sky was the very seeds from the dandelions in the valley and with that he had a strong urge to go into the valley, but he held back the urge as maybe not all was what it seemed in this beautiful land but as he looked across at Takt he saw his companion starting out down the hill, turning and beckoning Thaddeus to follow which he quickly did, his steps falling quickly on the soft and long grass until he caught up to his friend.

They soon reached the bottom of the hill and stood in awe as the valley around them stunned each of them with its magical setting. The mist that hugged the tree bases now curled around their feet, the branches hung low overhead with the bright petals of the flowers glowing in the sunlight that shone through them like piercing spears. They walked forward being careful where they stepped in case they trod on a flower, they hadn't been walking long until they saw the valley dip down, this surprised Thaddeus and Takt who hadn't spoken for what seemed like long minutes as when they stood at the peak the hill they could not see the dip in the land. They walked forward and saw that the trees that were so curly and twisted with their thick trunks protruding from the land acted as a barrier to the indentation in the ground which the travelers could now see was full of dandelions that looked like a large white carpet atop the grass.

"Where are we?" asked Thaddeus, his voice drifting off as he took in the sight before him, "I believe we are in the Dandelion Fields, it is where we will find the next piece of the Todesfall Clock" with those last words Thaddeus became slightly nervous as the last challenge they faced regarding the clock was extremely dangerous so thinking of what they may have to achieve in the pleasant looking field before them made Thaddeus tense. "Do you know what is in this field?" asked Thaddeus with a slight

quiver in his voice, "The fairies live
here" responded Takt as he began to
clamber through the thick branches of the
trees that stood before them and left
Thaddeus slightly stunned, "Fairies?" he
asked but received no response and decided
to see for himself as he clambered over
the thick branch that hung low to the
ground. When he had hopped over he stood
and gazed at the small valley in from of
him, he walked forward and started down
the small groove in the ground that seemed
to sink about ten feet into the earth, as
Thaddeus reached the bottom he saw Takt
ahead walking slowly through the thick
white dandelion carpet, a haze rose up
around his companion, the land around him
looking like its own secluded world that
no one would know about even if they came
within a few feet of it. The air was warm
here with a pleasant smell of thick grass
and plant life, there was also a mist that
swirled through the air which felt cool on
Thaddeus' skin as he moved forward and
followed Takt's footsteps through the
dandelions. It wasn't long before he
caught up to his friend who was stood
motionless looking around the ground like
he had lost something.

"What are you looking for Takt?" asked
Thaddeus as he also looked around the
ground, "From what I learnt from the books
and writings Gideon kept in the attic, the
Fairies which dwell within the Dandelion

Fields live close to the ground, they blend in to their surroundings as their skin can change color," started Takt before a small voice could be heard coming from somewhere in the air before them, "You know your Fairies" it said as Thaddeus and Takt looked around quickly for the source of the voice, "Who said that" said Thaddeus, "I did" it quickly responded but this time it came from behind them, Thaddeus turned quickly but still could not see anything, "Are you a Fairy?" asked Takt as he too looked around quickly, their voices were the only sound within the small valley within a valley, not even a bird could be heard, "I am" the small voice said and Thaddeus thought it sounded slightly like a small bird call, "Well, where are you?" asked Thaddeus as his voice slightly raised with frustration, "I am right in front of you, can't you see me?" The Fairy asked and with that Thaddeus saw a small something move in front of his eyes and when he let his eyes rest on whatever was moving he finally saw the Fairy, he couldn't believe what he was seeing as he grabbed blindly for Takt who was still glancing around for the location of the voice but as he felt Thaddeus' hand he looked up and instantly saw what his friend was looking at. The Fairy fluttered in front of Thaddeus' face, its skin changed to a pale brown color and Thaddeus could see its eyes which were large but without pupils or even color, they were an off-white color and seemed to protrude slightly from its small head in order for better vision Thaddeus imagined. Its body seemed thin and frail and its clothes looked like coiled vines which were wrapped around its torso and partly around its legs and arms, its arms were thin and its hands only had four fingers which were long and twig like. It was hard for Thaddeus to make any clear definition on the creature as it was incredibly small. But the Fairy's head seemed round which made its eyes look even larger and attached to its head were two large ears that bent around the shape of the head and pointed off of the top of the head in two curled points. Then Thaddeus noticed how the Fairy was flying, two tree leaves were flapping behind the little being which seemed to keep him in flight. "So, who are you?" asked the Fairy as it flew close to Thaddeus' eyes, peering at him with a little smile which seemed like the smallest of smiles that Thaddeus had ever seen and with the Fairy's question Thaddeus and Takt told of their quest, their journey so far and what they were in search of. "Well glad to meet you Thaddeus and Takt, I am Fadfin Flieger, pleased to meet you and that is a great tale you just told, I am sure my people could aid you in your quest" stated the Fairy, "Really?" asked Thaddeus in amazement, he didn't think that the Fairy would be willing to help them so easily but he didn't want to argue and said "That's great, thank you Fadfin" and with that Fadfin reached into a small bag that hung around his shoulder and drew out a small green substance that neither Thaddeus nor Takt could see what exactly it was, "Eat this" said Fadfin the Fairy and held out his small hand and floated towards the mouth of Thaddeus who opened his mouth before he could taste something bland but at the same time taste something a little bitter on his tongue. He closed his eyes and at the same time the Fairy floated towards Takt and placed his hand inside the ticking, clicking and winding mouth of the clockwork traveler, resting the substance onto a cog within the mouth of Takt the fairy floated back and said "Now close your eyes and chew but whatever you do, do not open your eyes unless you want to vomit yourself to death" Thaddeus froze for a moment but then, clamping his eyes even tighter shut he began to chew, he frantically mashed up the bitter tasting thing that was within his mouth but realized nothing was happening, he wondered if Takt was experiencing the same problem and just as he was about to disobey the Fairy and open his eyes, he felt different and then a wind blew across him as though he was falling but without leaving the ground. He had a sense that things were growing around him and like the very landscape had enlarged by a hundred times. Thaddeus didn't dare to open his eyes but something was urging him to, he didn't know why but he gently opened his eyes to see what was surrounding him and if he had fallen into a trap, his eyes opened and he saw… Takt, Takt was looking right at him and he was smiling but it took a moment for Thaddeus to realize what his friend was so happy about until he looked past him and saw that the Fairy, Fadfin Flieger was stood watching them also with a smile on his face only now he was the same size as they were, in fact he stood a little taller than Thaddeus and when Thaddeus looked around he saw that the dandelions which were hugging their shoes not a moment before were now towering above them, they stood to at least a hundred feet above them maybe even more, their large, round, white and fluffy heads swaying gently in the breeze that was absent at this low level.

They were stood in a large open space; the stems to the dandelions now looked like long smooth tree trunks that had a shine to them as the now even more distant sun bounced off of them. The ground was largely bumpy with gravel and earth that would have been near invisible a moment before was now the size of rocks and boulders. Thaddeus looked around in awe as the sight overwhelmed him, "Amazing isn't it?" asked Takt, "Wha- how? How did you do it" Asked Thaddeus in utter amazement, "How did I shrink you?" asked Fadfin

Flieger, "Well it was easy, I made you eat something called Moth Moss which is what shrunk you, I know it doesn't taste very appealing but it gets the job done" he explained as he led the amazed pair through some now large sprouting weeds and over a fallen twig that must have been fifty feet long, they dodged past some curling leaves that had long since fallen from the trees above which were now so far away and so tall it felt impossible to think they would ever be able to touch one of the branches, The air was cool around them with how low they were now to the ground and the moisture in the air was now large droplets of water which hung to petals and leaves overhead. The leaves and petals created a dense canopy which arched over the three of them, now deep in conversation about what had just happened, "So how do you we get back to our regular size?" asked Thaddeus, "It's easy" said Fadfin "you just need to eat some more of the Moth Moss, but it's much easier to shrink you then it is for us to grow bigger, on account of appearance and such" The Fairy said which Thaddeus thought didn't make much sense. Fadfin continued to lead them through the plant life, a creaking could be heard from the swaying dandelion stems as they passed underneath as well as distant cracks and rumbles from unknown sources.

"Where are you taking us?" asked Takt as he quickly walked along side Fadfin, "To my village, I think you are going to like it" he said and with that he pulled back a large overhanging petal to reveal a larger open space than the one they had just ventured from, within it were many wooden staircases that wound around the large stems of the dandelions and into the white cloud-like heads that towered above. Within the white masses could be seen small glowing lights that also littered the edges of the staircases. High above were fluttering shapes which Thaddeus couldn't seem to make out, as he trailed the staircases with his eyes he could see more Fairies moving up and down the winding stairs. At ground level there were small crooked huts that had small bright flowers wound into the thatched roofs with tiny glowing lights that shone out of the small oval windows. Small paths led up to different huts and Thaddeus thought it really did look like a small village with lights that were strung onto twig like poles which stuck out of the ground crookedly along different paths and trails, some led through the dandelions and were soon lost from sight in the dimming light, others led around the area in which they were looking and joined to the huts that scattered the area.

Above them high in the dandelions were small twinkling lanterns that seemed to

float in rows from one plant to another,
they looked like small stars and seeing
them gave Thaddeus a great feeling of
happiness that he was longing for, he had
no idea what the nature of the Fairies was
or what they would do to them but he
realized he just liked the setting he
stood within and wanted to see more of it.
"Follow me" said Fadfin as he walked
forward, the light bouncing of the Fairy's
light colored skin making it seem slightly
see through as he moved. Thaddeus and Takt
ran after him and were soon walking
through the Fairy village, walking around
different sized pieces of broken grass
that gave each hut a little privacy from
the others. They were in the very heart of
the small community within minutes and as
Thaddeus looked up he saw where the little
curly steps that ran up the dandelions led
to, there were the same small huts which
were at ground level attached to the sides
of dandelions with some hidden within the
white and fluffy heads, they seemed to
hang with the seeds as their small glowing
windows hung like starlight in the now
darkening sky. Thaddeus then realized
something, this being when he had first
seen Fadfin floating in front of him he
had not seemed this small, he had at least
seemed the size of a bee or wasp but now
they were all at least the size of small
specs that would be invisible to a regular
sized human being, this puzzled him and he
decided to question Fadfin about it, in

which he replied "Well before I venture out on scouting missions I eat some of the Moth Moss and it allows me to grow slightly otherwise the elements up there would surely destroy me in an instant" "How do you grow when eating the Moth Moss when it allowed us to shrink?" asked Thaddeus, "Well the Moth Moss does what it thinks needs to be done, in my instance I need to grow and in your instances you needed to shrink so that is what happened" replied Fadfin before continuing "But come quickly, our leader is desperate to meet you" and with that Fadfin hurried ahead before Thaddeus or Takt could ask any more questions. They hurried through the village and past the small huts which now seemed vacant, they came to a small bridge that arched upwards with small wooden slats, underneath was a stream that Thaddeus thought must have just been a trickle when he and Takt were regular size, they crossed before coming to a trail that led to steps, many steps that led upwards towards a purple flower that had more huts situated within it and at its centre was an ornate wooden building that had about four floors with a large pointed roof. Thaddeus could see glowing orange light that seeped from the small windows like little glowing embers, much like the houses that littered the ground below the large purple flower and like the small houses that hung high above. They began to climb the stairs which wound

around in different directions to avoid
the bent petals that curled overhead, they
soon reached the top and Thaddeus saw many
Fairies peering out of windows before
quickly closing the wooden shutters to
hide themselves, this small part of the
village towered above the rest of the huts
down below and also seemed different to
Takt and Thaddeus in the way that it was
much more ornate, with intricate carvings
embedded into the walls and doors that
surrounded with the lighting coming from
curled metal rods that housed glowing orbs
which shone brightly in the dimming light.
The lights led to the tall house which now
appeared to Thaddeus to be more of a
wooden mansion compared to the rest of the
huts. They moved closer with Fadfin taking
the lead, occasionally nodding at some of
the Fairies who watched from the doorways
of the wooden huts on either side of the
path leading to the wooden flower mansion.
They came to the main door and as Fadfin
pushed Thaddeus saw what was within the
building and this amazed him and Takt
instantly. Stood above him on balconies
that stretched above on all four floors
were hundreds of Fairies of all different
shapes and sizes, their large white eyes
stared down at the travelers and as Fadfin
led them ahead and up a large flight of
stairs they came upon the first floor
which more Fairies stood upon, some hiding
behind each other and some coming slightly
forward to get a better look at Thaddeus

and Takt, smiles creasing their round
heads like cracks in porcelain as small
hands reached tentatively towards them
before Fadfin pulled them on.

They climbed another flight of stairs,
then another and as they climbed Thaddeus
saw how the railings that guarded them
from the long drop were becoming more and
more ornate, like metallic ivy. The
lighting hung above them but not by ropes
or brackets but by nothing, they floated
in the centre of the large stairwell like
small suns, the light was golden and warm
and made Thaddeus feel welcome as he
noticed how the walls had carved imagery
of plants and trees embedded into the wood
that held the large house together.
Thaddeus wondered how this type of place
could possibly go unseen by humans that
may pass this way and he thought he would
need to ask about it when he next got
chance. They soon came to the top floor,
the roof was low and moss covered which
hung down in places like green spider webs
and with this Thaddeus was reminded for a
moment of the moss that lived within the
bog that Bolgreena inhabited. He never
wanted to see that place again and felt
happy that he was in a place such as the
Fairy Dandelion Village. They walked
forward and past more Fairies who now
seemed to have neater clothing on although
it was still bound ivy and leaves, they
now had a different look to the rest of

the Fairies that dwelled on the lower
floors. They passed through a door and
into a large room that had a long table
within it, the table looked like a piece
of bark and made Thaddeus and Takt wonder
if it actually was, being that they were
now extremely small the table in front of
them could well be a piece of worn bark,
its color was a deep brown with long dark
cracks that ran through its centre, it had
moss that hung from it underneath and sat
at the head of it was a tall looking
Fairy, he had the same large eyes without
any pupils or color, his skin was a darker
tone than Fadfin and protruding from his
head were two horns that looked like deer
antlers but under closer inspection
actually seemed to be branches that sprung
out in different directions, they were
worn and very crooked looking which gave a
sense of age to the big Fairy. The older
looking Fairy stood as the travelers
approached and his mouth creased to a
smile, "Thaddeus Loveguard and Takt
Zifferblatt, it is so good to finally meet
you" he said and came forward to embrace
the now shocked looking pair, "I am sorry
sir, but how do you know us?" asked Takt
in still amazement, "I know all about your
quest, but do you know all about your
quest?" The Fairy asked before barking
into a sharp laugh, his voice was deep and
bellowing but it did not suite his frame,
he was tall, much taller than Thaddeus,
Takt or even Fadin, he towered above them

but his body was thin and crooked looking like he was starting to turn into the wood that surrounded them and with that Thaddeus couldn't help but again compare the similarities between the Fairy and the Witch, but the Fairy was much more welcoming and so was the setting they stood within with a warm glow to the room as well as a nice heat that flowed from an open fire behind the tall Fairy. The larger Fairy wore deep red clothing that twisted around his limbs like an elegant silk but this was not silk, "Ah, I see you noticing my appearance, and you would be interested to know this new attire is actually made from spider silk, would you believe it? Once enemies now making clothing for me, incredible! But come and sit with me" and with that he turned and sat at his table beckoning Thaddeus, Takt and Fadfin to sit at the closest available seats.

"My name is Feen Lowenzahn, I am king of this particular realm of Fairies and I have been for the last four-hundred and thirty-six years, your quest is greatly known within the Fairy world and I imagine it is within all of the Creature world," "How is that?" asked Takt, "How could it not be my clockwork friend? You are looking for the Todesfall Clock, the most precious of items within our world but unfortunately lost many, many centuries ago, do you know that if the clock is

remade it could allow the dead to be
visible once again? for only a short while
bear in mind, but it could allow kings to
gather wisdom from past kings, it could
allow the swapping of knowledge and power
but it must be in the right hands, the
creatures that dwell within the Malimar
want the clock so they can raise their
armies of evil, but if the clock is
possessed and fixed by a person with the
purest of heart and greatest of intentions
then it will keep the Malimar occupants at
bay and send all of the others back within
the Ink World for the rest of eternity as
it is known some of them have… escaped
into this realm. The clock is much more
valuable then you could possibly imagine"
stated Feen Lowenzahn to three stunned
faces. Thaddeus hadn't known of the power
the clock possessed and after looking over
at Takt he realized that his companion had
no idea either.

"The tales can wait until later, please,
eat something" said Feen nearly shouting
with his bellowing voice and when Thaddeus
looked down he saw that there was food on
the large bark table in front of him,
there was food that he actually liked,
steaks and potatoes as well as Yorkshire
pudding with carrots and when Thaddeus
looked up at Feen in amazement he saw the
Fairy leader cast him a wink and a smile.
Thaddeus dug in to the food not really
caring how he looked, he hadn't eaten

properly in the weeks they had been travelling, all he had eaten was tins of mackerel and raw potatoes from fields they had passed by and as he eat he felt so much better, his aches and pains seemed to ease, he drank from the curly goblet that sat before him and was filled with a delicious type of ale which he quickly gulped down without missing a drop and carried on eating from the large plate filled with food. He had soon finished and sat back with his stomach full and satisfied, he looked over to see Feen and Takt talking over the pieces of maps and notes that Gideon Lilleyman had scribbled and saw they were examining each part with great concentration, "So this map has all of the locations in which the pieces of the clock can be found?" asked Feen as he looked up at Takt and peered through his small oval spectacles, "We believe so, well it has aided us well so far, we have no other way of locating the clock other than these maps and also the directions we have been given" said Takt as his glowing eyes drifted away for a moment with the thought of the Man of the Corn and of Bolgreena.

"Ah, well your choice to venture here was the right choice but now I believe we can leave our discussion until the morning, your journey will not be impeded as time is different in our world" stated Feen Lowenzahn as he stood, towering over the

still sitting travelers before they joined
him and stood, "You may be interested to
know…" continued Feen as he began to walk
towards a large door at the rooms rear
which had beautiful carvings of creatures
that resembled some form of angel, "That
we do have a piece of the clock you are
looking for, we have kept it safe for over
a century, you seem as though your
intentions are good but tomorrow I require
a task from you, all will be explained
tomorrow whilst breakfast is served, if
you succeed we will give you the piece of
the Todesfall Clock as you would have
proved your dedication, but now please
allow Fadfin to show you to your rooms and
please feel free to walk around our ground
but please do not venture past the line of
dandelion stems" and with that Feen
Lowenzahn had exited the room through the
large carved door and was gone with a
number of well dressed Fairies quickly
following behind. Thaddeus and Takt stood
for a moment in awe of the large Fairy
King before Fadfin spoke, "My friends,
please follow me as I will show you to
your accommodation" It took a moment for
the two friends to register that Fadfin
had even said anything but they soon came
back down to earth before turning, smiling
at each other and walking with Fadfin.

They walked behind the Fairy who led them
up and down flights of twisting stairs,
they climbed steeply but could not see

where about they were walking to but then suddenly they came out onto a long balcony, the balcony stretched into the dandelions high above the village they were in almost an hour previous. They walked along the walkway which had a twisted railing that seemed to be made from thistle thorns and twisted nettle leaves which were all tightly wound together, on the right of them were small doorways which seemed to be made from the same material that the rest of village huts were made from, they were attached to a long wooden wall which Thaddeus believed to have small rooms behind as a faint glow shone from underneath the doorways. Soon enough Thaddeus' beliefs were confirmed as they stopped with Fadfin outside of two small doors, both matching the ones they had just passed. Fadfin twisted a vine that was wrapped around the door handle and opened it; he then proceeded to do the same to the next door before again, opening it. "Here you are Thaddeus" said Fadfin as he pointed to the first room they stood in front of, "And Takt, this is your room" said the Fairy as he guided Takt Zifferblatt to the next room, Thaddeus found himself momentarily alone in the small and glowing room, the light shone from a little lantern that sat in the corner next to a bed made of a large leaf and stood on small broken twigs, the walls seemed crooked as the wooden twigs that made them stood crookedly with the

ivy that strung them together. The floor
was the same as the walls but seemed very
solid as Thaddeus stepped onto it, the
lantern stood atop a dried out baby
mushroom, the color of it was a dark brown
and seemed to be varnished somehow but
Thaddeus thought it complemented the room
nicely. There was a pebble that acted as a
table in the centre of the room and at its
rear was a form of tubing which Thaddeus
soon realized was a rolled up grass leaf
which was spearing through the wall and
into a large, upside down snail shell that
had small paintings all over it, the
previous occupant of the room must have
had the need of a little decoration and
had painted on what must be a form of
sink, bubbling out of the rolled up grass
leaf was a drop of water but was now the
size of Thaddeus' head as he was now
shrunk to tiny proportions. He moved into
the room and sat on the bed for a moment,
it felt comfortable and the overall warmth
of the room made Thaddeus feel extremely
welcome but also slightly sleepy as he
gazed past the door into the now dark
beyond.

Takt came in suddenly through the dark
opening with a large smile on his stitched
and clockwork face, "Isn't this place
amazing?" stated the clockwork creation in
excitement, he sat next to Thaddeus who
smiled at his friend, "It is the land of
dreams" replied Thaddeus as he stood, Takt

followed as they both stepped out onto the long walkway, they leant on the blunt thistle railing and gazed into the dark dandelion forest, beyond they could see small lights glinting from the Fairy village. The railing they leant upon now glowed in the darkness as many lanterns that were attached to the railing shone in the night air giving inhabitants enough light to navigate the village which now seemed to Thaddeus to be more like a small city. Thaddeus liked the lights, he liked the setting that surrounded them it made him feel welcome and safe, he felt as though he could stay here forever and as though nothing could harm him here, the memories of Bolgreena, the Witch of the Maug and the memory of the Malimar in which Takt and himself had faced the thick and evil ooze and in the same place where they had faced the Jewel Box Dolls, all seemed so distant to him now. He liked it this way he thought as the pair stood for a moment, "This is turning out to be quite an adventure" said Thaddeus as he looked over at Takt who gave him a wide smile before they both started laughing, "I wonder what we will encounter next and I wonder what the task will be tomorrow" said Takt as he looked back out in to the darkness and the twinkling lantern lights, "I can't even imagine what it could be, or what the next part of the journey will be" replied Thaddeus as he too looked out into the darkness, "But I am glad we are doing this together Takt, I don't think I could have done this alone, I owe you a lot my friend" continued Thaddeus as he looked back at his companion, and as Takt looked over at his friend he replied, "I wouldn't have gotten far without you either Thaddeus, and whatever we face next I am glad we will face it together" and with that they both smiled at each other, "I think I best get some sleep" said Thaddeus before turning for his small, wooden room, "Ok my friend, you sleep well and tomorrow we will face whatever challenge is set for us" laughed Takt as Thaddeus entered his room, closing the little wooden door behind him and leaving his companion stood against the railing before lying down on the surprisingly comfortable bed. It wasn't long before Takt returned to dwell upon the next day's task but before long his mind became tired, Takt was indeed dead and had possessed the clockwork doll that could now easily move but his mind still became weary and he fell into a trance like state, the doll remained still as he seemingly shut down and remained still as his mind prepared for the next day.

12.

A Journey by Dandelion.

Thaddeus awoke from a deep sleep suddenly, he had rested very well and felt refreshed as he hadn't slept much in the past couple of weeks that they had been travelling, and to finally place his head on a pillow felt great even if it was made of moss. He sat up and stretched before glancing at the doorway, light spilled underneath the crack at the bottom of the wooden door and a shadow could be seen moving and just as Thaddeus stood a knock sounded from the entrance to his small Fairy room. He walked over still slightly uneasy on his tired legs, he opened the door to find Fadfin looking at him with a wide smile on his round Fairy face, "Hello Thaddeus, sleep well?" said Fadfin, straightening as he said it to appear more important which Thaddeus thought he definitely was, "Hello Fadin" replied Thaddeus, "I slept very well thank you" he continued as he stepped out into the bright light that was filtering through the dandelion seeds above. Takt was stood to his right looking out at the view from the balcony, his expression was that of someone who deep in concentration but as he saw Thaddeus exit his room a smile creased his clockwork face, "Hello there Thaddeus" said Takt, "Hiya Takt" replied Thaddeus cheerfully. "Shall we proceed to the dining hall? Feen Lowenzahn wishes to speak with you both over breakfast" asked Fadfin and with that Thaddeus nodded to his friend who responded with a confident nod and they both followed Fadfin towards the dining hall. They walked down the spiraled stairs they had traveled up the night before and soon they were stood in the large hall with the bark table, at the head of it was sat Feen Lowenzahn, a wide smile across his large head with the two branch horns that rose above like wooden lightning bolts. He stood as they approached and his bellowing voice rang out across the long bark table, "Good morning my friends, I trust you slept well, please come and join me as we discuss things" and as he spoke Thaddeus and Takt moved forward to sit on either side of the table and next to the tall Fairy king. Feen looked at them both and smiled, he leant back in the large wooden chair that looked like dead wood with its pale tone and worn look, "I shall not keep you waiting as I know you must be eager to know what I will ask of you" said Feen, "We are indeed your majesty" said Takt and with that the king chuckled, "Please you may call me Feen, and without any further delay I shall tell you the challenge that is requested of you, you see there has been a war that has raged for the past millennia it is between the Fairies and the Pixies" started Feen before Thaddeus spoke looking stunned in his seat, "Pixies?, like the Pixies that play pranks?" he asked "Those are the Pixies that are known in your world through stories and fairytales Thaddeus, the Pixies that really exist are much more fierce, they are like Fairies but are more animalistic but also very co-ordinated which makes them extremely dangerous, they live in large numbers but luckily there are many more Fairies that can come to each other's aid quite easily, but the Pixies know the element of surprise and can strike before our scouts have time to see them. They have killed many of our clans" said Feen as he looked downwards, his face casting a slight grimace and his large colorless eyes seemed to fill with tears before he continued, "They were once Fairies but something changed within them, some rumors say that the Ink Twins from the Malimar cast a spell over them which turned them into the dark race of Pixies that have been our enemies for so long" said Feen, "The Ink Twins?" asked Takt "The Ink Twins are dark creatures that used to dwell within the Malimar, some say that they were the kings of that oozing world but they now reside somewhere in the human world, they are made of the very slime that the Malimar drips with, they are pure evil that cast off pollution from their festering bodies, but I have a feeling that you may encounter them a long your travels, but that is not what we must discuss now" said Feen before he continued, but Thaddeus didn't listen for a moment because of the feeling of dread that swam through him so swiftly it left him cold. The Ink Twins only needed to be spoken of to entice fear and Thaddeus couldn't help but be reminded of the inky slime that chased them on their brief journey into the Malimar, and what did Feen mean by the fact that they may encounter them? But Thaddeus pushed the feeling of dread aside and listened to what Feen had to say.

"There is a jewel" was the next part of the conversation that Thaddeus heard Feen Lowenzahn say, "A jewel that if placed into an ancient rock which the Fairies have possessed since the beginning of time, it will allow the race of Fairies all over the world to become truly hidden from the rest of the world, including all creatures mythical, we will become invisible like we once were" said the large king, "How did you lose possession of the jewel?" asked Takt as Thaddeus added to the question, "And I am guessing that you were once hidden from the world but not anymore?" "That is right Thaddeus, we were once invisible to all, it allowed us to build our villages and homes in places we could never build them now, we could build our structures in the trees

and the magic we possessed allowed humans
and other creatures to not feel the need
to approach the area we lived in. Other
creatures would just avoid us and the area
around us, it was extremely useful but
alas, the magic was taken from us in the
form of the jewel I spoke of, it was taken
by a small group of Pixies that were
trained especially in the art of thievery
and one night they located the jewel which
rested on top of a black oak staff, they
broke the staff and took the jewel. But
now the rock has been discovered, the
jewel is called the Moak Crone Pearl and
was formed from the Moak rock, to combine
them both will mean they can never be
taken apart again and will always give
protection to the Fairy world in whatever
they need." Thaddeus and Takt looked on,
neither of them had ever heard of the Moak
Crone Pearl but the idea of it was
intriguing that Thaddeus wished to see the
Pearl and to feel or even see its power,
he had an inclination of what Feen wanted
them to do, "You need us to find the pearl
don't you?" Thaddeus asked, "Oh no my
friend, I do not need you to find the
pearl, as I already know where it is"
replied Feen.

Thaddeus and Takt looked surprised, they
stared at each other before hearing the
deep voice of the Fairy king speak and
tell them what they were waiting to hear,
"It resides on Trummelboot Hill, there is

a tree atop of it called the Roterbaum tree, it is ancient but covering the red bark is a layer of Moth Moss and even though we use Moth Moss greatly within our world, it is what is within the Moth Moss that we are concerned with, as on the north side of the tree, beneath the Moss is a hole in the trunk of the tree, within that cavity is the Moak Crone Pearl" said Feen, "Where can this hill with the tree be found?" asked Takt, "It is located to the east of this village, through the gap in the surrounding valley hills which once you pass through you will be able to see your destination in the distance, but there are things you must know before, the Trummelboot hill is home to a troll, hence the name "Trummel". Trummel trolls are related to woodland trolls but dwell within countryside's and grasslands, they are extremely good at blending in to their surroundings and this is the reason we have never even seen the troll" said Feen, "If you have never seen it, how do you know it even exists?" asked Thaddeus as he drunk from the curled goblet containing now some very tasty juice which Thaddeus had never tasted before, it had a hint of blueberries and also chocolate. "We know because within the Roterbaum Tree live the Pixies we fight against, they have built their village high above in the branches, they have threatened us in the past saying if we do not hand our territory over to them and become slaves to them and the

Malimar then they will awaken the troll and make it destroy us. We know these are empty threats as they do not know exactly where our village is, or where any other Fairy village is for that matter but their scouts draw closer each day so I fear we are running out of time, will you help us in return for the piece of the Todesfall clock?" asked Feen which sounded to Thaddeus and Takt more like a plead, a hint of fear and also desperation was present in the large Fairy's deep and booming voice, the long fingers of the king constantly twitched and picked at the edge of the table in nervousness and anticipation. Thaddeus looked around the room and saw that no more than thirty Fairy's had quietly entered through the large doors and into the room which was now filled with a bright light that spilled through the large open window which was not made from glass but actually from wings, from insect wings in fact. Thaddeus thought it must be from the wings of a dragonfly due to the many small veins and lines that ran through the thin wing, it made the light that filtered through a very slight orange or beige color. Thaddeus looked over at the Fairies that were crowded together waiting for the travelers answer, their faces were small and round and on a few of the older looking fairies their faces were lined and cracked looking, like dried up leaves with beards that looked more like squashed spider webs. The clothing on them varied, ranging from long elegant robes that looked similar to what Feen was wearing, some looked more like Fadfin as small plant vines were wrapped tightly around them but what was similar in all of them was the nervous look on their faces which Thaddeus felt he didn't want them to show much longer, and with that he looked over at Takt who smiled slightly then they both looked at an equally nervous looking Feen Lowenzahn, and together they both spoke, "We will help you" and with that Feen burst into a loud laugh that sounded more like a cheer and as he stood with arms the rest of the Fairies burst into a cheer that rang through the room and seemed to make the crooked walls shake. Thaddeus looked around with a wide smile on his face and he realized that the room looked almost like a nest, the walls that had been hidden partly in shadow the night before now looked twisted and bound together in the twigs that made up the rooms that Thaddeus and Takt had slept in the night before. The large room they stood within now looked more round than it did before but Thaddeus then thought more about the task they were about to embark on. The sound of the cheers and laughter as well as the hard patting on his back from the surrounding Fairies that had crowded around the pair seemed to die away as he thought of what they might face, but whatever it was and however dangerous it may be there would be a reward at the end of it, this being that they would be one step closer to finding all of the pieces of the clock, one more piece after the ones the Fairies held and he could see his beloved Pandora again. This thought gave Thaddeus renewed drive to complete the quest, a drive that had ebbed away during their adventure due to fatigue and lack of food, but he was now fully restored and eager to set on his way with his friend at his side, to find the Moak Crone Pearl and help the world of Fairies.

The Fairies had cheered for them, they shook hands with them allowing Thaddeus to feel the cool and rough skin on the hands of the Fairies, Feen grasped both Thaddeus and Takt by the shoulders and took them away from the small crowd which turned in discussion with one another, the tall king opened the dragonfly window and allowed them to peer outside, a long way below in the village they had both passed through the night before were hundreds of Fairies, all cheering at Thaddeus and Takt, the news had traveled quickly and now all over the flower heads and high above in the dandelion heads were cheers, cheers that rang through the large hall they stood within, but Takt turned suddenly, "I think we should be on our way as soon as possible" he said through his clockwork mouth, Feen Lowenzahn's face turned from a smile to suddenly stern, "Very well, the sooner you are on your way the sooner you will return, Fadfin will go with you, he knows the way and can aid you greatly" and with the king's words Fadfin appeared at their sides, he held in his hands the belt that Thaddeus kept his screwdrivers and small hammer, he also held the satchel that contained the maps and notes of Gideon Lilleyman as well as the first piece of the clock. "Thank you" said Thaddeus as he fastened the belt around his waist and took the satchel with which he secured it over his shoulder, tightened the buckles and straps before straightening and looking at Takt and the two Fairies, "Ready?" he said with which Feen laughed loudly, "I admire your eagerness my human friend" said Feen as Takt walked over to Thaddeus, Fadfin stood readily awaiting the two travelers and with a quick nod to Feen, the three departed. They slipped through the still cheering crowd of Fairies leaving the tall Fairy king looking out at the village he watched over with his long arms held firmly behind his back.

The three travelers walked down the wide and open staircases that Thaddeus and Takt had walked up the night before after entering the palace that rested upon the bright flower. This time there were only a few Fairies that were walking in all different directions, some holding peculiar items, one Fairy was walking ahead of them with her arms held out and her palms facing upwards, floating just a couple of inches above her open hands were three purple balls, they floated around each other with a faint blue mist that hung closely to the spheres, Thaddeus was quite amazed at the sight, he looked over the railing that lined the wide stairs as they traveled downwards and was amazed as equally as the night before at how magical the building they were in actually was. Light flowed through a large window that Thaddeus imagined was another insect wing, the illumination from outside bounced down the winding stairwell, Thaddeus could see the light particles which danced and flurried off the walls, darting off glowing objects that Thaddeus had never seen before, he was filled with a feeling of happiness just like he was the night before as he stood outside of the room he was to sleep in, but the realization of the day ahead shook him and he was filled once again with determination, he hurried after Takt and Fadfin who were a few paces ahead and as he caught up Takt threw him a smile and a wink.

They reached the bottom of the stairwell but instead of passing through the large wooden door that stood in front of them and opened onto the large flower head, they instead rounded at the bottom step and headed in the opposite direction to the door. Neither Thaddeus nor Takt

questioned this as they knew that the
Fairy that was to accompany them would
take them the way they needed to go. They
walked down a long passageway which was
much more narrow than the open staircase
they were just on, it had a crooked
ceiling that seemed to bend in the middle,
there were doorways that lined each wall,
leaves and petals were bound into the
wooden wall on each side which Thaddeus
thought to be a form of decoration. There
were small glowing orbs like the ones that
floated around the building during the
night, they floated like small stars down
the passageway and gave off a warm, golden
glow. Suddenly Fadfin stopped, unwound the
vine that wrapped around the handle of the
little wooden door, opened it and stepped
through. Thaddeus got a sense of urgency
from the movements of the Fairy, "Where do
you think he is taking us?" asked Thaddeus
to his companion, "I have no idea but the
best thing we can do would be to trust him
and just see where we end up" replied
Takt, "I agree" said Thaddeus as the three
of them stepped into a room that was small
and round, small twigs rounded the entire
length of the room giving it a definite
nest feel. There was nothing else in the
room but a small wooden trapped door in
the centre of the floor, it was oval in
shape and a deep brown color, the wooden
pieces that made the little door had small
gaps in but beyond it looked dark and
Thaddeus felt a sense of fear briefly rush

through him, but as Fadin knelt down, his
boney looking knee resting on the floor
and his long fingers opening the trap door
carefully, Thaddeus swallowed his fear
down and stepped forward wanting to see
what awaited them, Fadfin looked up at
them both, "Do not be afraid, this passage
leads to the dandelions, we are in need of
transportation so I need to meet with an
old friend, so please follow me" and with
that the Fairy had vanished down into the
passageway. Thaddeus and Takt looked at
each other, "Are you scared?" asked Takt,
"Yes" replied Thaddeus as he looked down
at the dark opening in the ground, "We are
in this together Thaddeus, whatever
happens I am here and we will get through
it together" said Takt as he placed a hand
on Thaddeus' shoulder, Thaddeus looked at
his friend and smiled, he felt the fear
that clung to him disappear, "I am glad
you are here Takt" said Thaddeus as he
moved towards the hole, "And I you, watch
your head and I will be right behind you"
and with that Thaddeus stepped into the
open passageway and moved downwards. The
passage was narrow and Thaddeus noticed
that it suddenly had a damp feel to it as
well as the walls having a green coloring,
Thaddeus rested his hand upon the wall to
steady himself as he moved down the narrow
and winding staircase and felt the damp
texture, the wall was ridged and bumpy
with a moisture that seemed to just be
water but the droplets seemed much larger

which Thaddeus thought was due to the size the travelers had been shrunk to. Thaddeus soon heard Takt moving behind him which gave him a reassuring feel, "This is a strange place" said Takt with a slight chuckle in his voice, "I wonder where we are" asked Thaddeus as the moved downwards, the passage seemed to become wider as the moved steeply downwards, they spiraled and spiraled as the descended, it seemed to take a long time but suddenly they came to an opening where Fadfin stood waiting for them, behind him sunlight shone brightly onto a landscape that was very green, "I thought you would never get here" said Fadfin as they exited the small opening, and then suddenly Thaddeus and Takt were once again stunned by what they saw, they were surrounded by the large dandelions that towered above them, they dominated the landscape in front of them and seemed to stretch on for miles but was probably only a few feet when they were normal size Thaddeus thought to himself.

"In front of you is the dandelion fields, the palace we were in a moment ago was the Dandelion House, it is the home of our king Feen Lowenzahn, we have just traveled down the stem underneath the Dandelion House to this place, it is where myself and the rest of the scouts travel to different locations including looking for the Pixie enemy and also for useful items" said Fadfin with a very proud tone to his voice, Thaddeus was still stunned at the landscape around them and realized that they were stood upon a large leaf that was attached to the flower with which the Dandelion House sat upon, "How do you travel from here?" asked Takt, "Ah, well we travel in either two ways, one is by the leaf wings that I actually invented and now most of the Fairy scouts within the Fairy world use, or the other way is by dandelion seeds, it is a little slower but much easier to maneuver" said Fadfin, Thaddeus then remembered something, "Wait a minute, when we were entering this land, we saw hundreds of dandelion seeds floating upwards and some surrounded us, were they Fairies?" he asked, "Yes some of them would have been, they were different families of Fairies that had either visited loved ones from other Fairy villages close by, or they were leaving to visit another village and see loved ones there, they travel by the seeds as to not draw attention from the Pixies that may be scouting nearby, as even though the Pixies do not know where we dwell, they could easily intercept the seeds which would give our location away," said Fadfin, "So how many other Fairy villages are there?" asked Thaddeus, "Oh, there are about thirty nearby, some much larger than our village, but across the entire country is hard to say, much less than there used to be that is for certain, but let's be on our way shall we?" said Fadfin as he moved closer to the edge of the leaf and started to look downwards, and then he whistled very loudly three times, he waited for a moment and then whistled three times further, his whistle sounded like a birdcall and was very tuneful. Fadfin turned to look back at Thaddeus and Takt, "I have to see a friend first, please don't be alarmed when he arrives, but just as he said that four enormous long, black legs reached over the edge of the leaf and pulled a large black body upwards, four more legs appeared and Thaddeus realized it was a giant spider that dwarfed all three of the travelers, its face held eight round and shiny eyes, it had large mandibles that twitched as it moved towards them slowly, its long black legs had spiky hairs that stuck out in all different directions and the rear of the spider was big and round and it swayed as the creature moved sideways but always kept the three of them in its view, Thaddeus was frozen and so was Takt, they couldn't move but noticed that Fadfin moved closer to the giant spider with a long smile on his face, "Hello Draedan" said Fadfin towards the large monster, but then something incredible happened, the spider spoke back to Fadfin, "Hello Fadfin, how have you been?" it said in a raspy but high toned voice, it sounded like air passing through leaves, it was crispy and rough but suited the beast, "Who do we have here?" it suddenly said without moving its body, one of the eight eyes must have spotted Thaddeus and Takt stood close to the opening of the stem, "I—I—We… we are…" stuttered Thaddeus, "Speak up my friend, my hearing is not as good as it once was" spoke the giant spider and with that it scuttled quickly towards them and peered its large round head at them both, "Ah, a human and, what are you my friend?" it said towards Takt who didn't have time to say anything "A Vormundgeist?" it said in a tone that sounded like surprise, Takt nodded but the spider looked back at Fadfin quickly who was still smiling, "The Todesfall Clock?" the spider asked with a gasp and with that Fadfin nodded in agreement. The spider looked back at the pair, its round black eyes staring, "You are on your way to find the clock of death?" asked the spider, Thaddeus could feel warm air blowing across his face, it was peculiar as it didn't actually smell like Thaddeus thought it would, it didn't really have a smell at all and neither did the large black body of the arachnid, it just looked foreboding as it stood looking down at him, "We are on this quest in order to see our loved ones one more time" said Thaddeus loudly, his neck craned upwards to match the spider's gaze, "Indeed you are, but your possessing the clock is more important than you could possible imagine, by the pair of you retrieving all its lost pieces and restoring it, you will return balance to the mythical world, you will cast the creatures of the Malimar back to where they crawled out of, the Todesfall Clock has more power than you could ever dream of and it is imperative that you find it" replied the large spider and then it looked over at its Fairy friend, "Are you travelling with them?" it asked Fadfin, "No I am just journeying with them to find the Moak Crone Pearl atop Trummelboot hill" said Fadfin, the spider then looked shocked, "You are venturing to where the Pixies dwell?" asked the spider with a hint of fear and anger in its voice, "The quest is too dangerous, you should have more Fairies with you, the Pixies alone have much larger numbers than the three of you! it is foolish for you to travel there" continued the spider now sounding extremely concerned, but Fadfin did not look phased and simply smiled at the large spider before saying "Ah but we have our Moth Moss, we plan on travelling to the old tree at Thaddeus and Takt's normal size" The spider then gasped before laughing loudly "Fairies do surprise me with their courage, you must take care though my friends, and please take this…" with that the spider reached behind its round head and removed a shining orb, it twinkled in the sunlight and seemed just like one of the orbs that gave the Fairies light within the Dandelion House, Takt took it in his clockwork hand and placed it in the satchel around Thaddeus' shoulder, "It is the Himliss Stone, it will protect you when you need it to so keep it close" Thaddeus was reminded of the power that resided within Takt Zifferblatt, he wondered if the power would show itself on the task for the Fairies that they were about to embark on, and he also wondered if they would be in need of it at all.

The spider moved away from them and towards the edge of the large green leaf they stood upon before it looked back at the three of them, "If you are to travel to the Trummelboot Hill then you will need transport" and with that the large spider disappeared over the side of the leaf, Takt and Thaddeus peered over the edge and saw an enormous web that was strung from stem to stem, it was thick white and made it difficult for either of them to see the ground, "The web protects our village, Draedan spun it many years ago when our friendship with the spiders was strong, before the spiders left due to the increasing threat of the Pixies" said Fadfin who was now stood at Takt's side and was also peering over the edge of the leaf. "Why did the spiders leave?" asked Thaddeus, "They left because the Pixies threatened them, they wanted the spiders to join them or they would start to destroy the habitats of the arachnids so in fear they left. Draedan only stayed because he had no family, he had nothing to lose so he stayed, he now supplies the transportation for travelling Fairies or scouts" said Fadfin and just as he said it, a shadow formed overhead and as all three of the waiting travelers looked up they saw the large body of Draedan lowering from the towering dandelion plants up above.

The spider lowered to the edge of the leaf by a thick and silvery strand of silk, it now being the thickness of rope and glistened in the sunlight. Wrapped up in webbing and attached to the side of the spider was three large dandelion seeds, the long and silver stems tied tightly together as the wiry tops to the seed looked almost halo-like as they protruded above the height of the spider, the long wisps spread in all different directions. The spider unwrapped the large seeds and placed one in front of each traveler, they floated there for a moment without once touching the leaf, the seeds were so light that they floated with the air that slightly breezed around all of them. Fadfin wasted no time and stepped onto the large dandelion seed, the weight of the Fairy only making the seed bob slightly in the air, Fadfin looked over and beckoned Thaddeus and Takt to take to their seeds which Takt soon did, a look of excitement creased across his face, Takt stepped onto the long piece of dandelion as it bobbed slightly just like their Fairy companion's

did. Thaddeus didn't waste any time and
moved forward to the last seed, he stepped
onto it and grabbed a hold of the stem, it
lowered with his weight but remained
floating above the green of the leaf, he
looked over at the other two who were
smiling at him and Takt looked truly
thrilled to be traveling in such a unique
way. Thaddeus felt exactly the same and
the nerves he had felt a moment before
were soon vanishing as he tightened his
grip on the silvery green stem, his
footing was sturdy and he felt safe stood
upon the seed and as he looked up he saw
the sunlight stream through the silver
parachute above. The breeze made the long
wisps sway gently and then Thaddeus heard
Fadfin speak, "You need to kick off from
the ground firmly and when we are in the
air just lean against the stem in the
direction you wish to travel in, if your
legs become tired then you can sit upon
the area in which you stand on and allow
your feet to dangle, make sure before we
depart that you pull a strand of the stem
and secure it around your wrist so you do
not fall off, ok are we ready? And off we
go" and with that Fadfin kicked off from
the large green leaf and was soon floating
above, Thaddeus pulled a strand of the
stem around his wrist, hopped one foot
onto the leaf and pushed, he was soon
floating upwards and as he looked
downwards he saw Takt begin to float
upwards and below him, stood on the large

green leaf was the spider looking upwards at them. Thaddeus waved at the spider before looking up to locate Fadfin who was floating only a few feet above, the stems of the dandelions around them moving past quickly as they ascended and soon they were amongst the bright white heads of the large plants, they passed bridges that connected the flowers and within the seed-covered heads were the many huts that Thaddeus had seen at ground level, Fairies waved from the windows of the huts and from the crooked bridges that were strung in every direction. From one plant to another, flags and decorations hung from the seeds that spiked the air from the large dandelions "In the summer the dandelions are bright yellow and they have petals instead of the seeds" shouted Fadfin from the seed above, Takt was now floating next to Thaddeus and as he looked over Takt sent him a warm smile and a wave, "How do you travel around if the dandelions have no seeds?" asked Thaddeus as he gained slightly on Fadfin in order to hear him better. "We collect them from the dandelions that surround the village, the ones we haven't used for our homes of course, we have Fairies that journey to neighboring plants and harvest the seeds, if we had continued down the stem from the Dandelion House then we would have come to where we keep hundreds of the seeds, all tied together waiting to be used and of course if we travel away on them we do try and bring them back" laughed Fadfin as they ascended higher still until suddenly rising above the dandelions. The breeze on Thaddeus' face was warm and refreshing as they floated through the calm air, the land looked beautiful as everything was so much larger it resembled something from a dream, the air was now visible somehow as particles of moisture now floated past them, ahead was now a mist that swirled around in magnificent curls and twists which seemed to make the air have a mind of its own. The tree that sat in the distance but Thaddeus knew would have only been a few feet away in his regular size, now seemed to be hundreds and hundreds of feet high. It lost definition from its great height as the sun filtered through the immensely thick branches, the light was golden and warm and as Thaddeus closed his eyes he felt at piece, there was not a worry in the world as he soared higher and sound was absent as they floated upwards which gave Thaddeus a sense of freedom and so much relaxation that he could of fallen asleep there and then. Fadfin looked over at the traveler and smiled and Takt felt just like Thaddeus did as peace ran through his stitched fabric body, he felt relaxed and also felt as though he had become attached to the clockwork body that Thaddeus had made, his spirit joining with the cogs and metal that made his created body. But with this journey they had embarked on he had started to feel some aches and pains albeit they were probably all in his mind but Takt didn't mind, he liked the feelings that reminded him of his previous life. The wind that passed through the fabric of his body made him happy and as he saw his friend and companion at utter peace he realized he felt the same, he felt good and real and he felt glad to be on the adventure they were on and felt even happier at the company he was keeping.

They had been traveling for what felt like a long time, Thaddeus was now sitting upon his seed and was looking around, he could see so much that his eyes had never seen before such as insects that were now twice the size of himself buzzing a long way above, the hum of their wings vibrating loudly through the air above. Thaddeus looked downwards and saw they were extremely high above the ground but somehow he didn't feel scared and he actually felt safe, then as he looked ahead he saw the ground rise into two hills that had a gap in the middle which looked like valley, it seemed enormous but Thaddeus knew it would have only been a few feet high at his regular size. Thaddeus looked ahead and saw Fadfin lean forward slightly on his dandelion stem and then suddenly gain speed, Thaddeus did the same and as he looked back at Takt he saw that his actions had been noticed as his friend was now speeding behind them. They picked up more speed as they caught a breeze underneath the parachute above, it felt exhilarating as they flew and then Thaddeus saw Fadfin look over his shoulder, "We need to pick up as much speed as possible to pass through the valley, there are warm pockets of air that stream from the mud below, if we are going too slow and get caught in one then we will be sent high into the air and the wind up there will certainly destroy us, it passes across the top of the two hills, do you see?" shouted Fadfin with one arm and hand extended towards the valley, Thaddeus and Takt looked hard ahead and then saw the wind, it was flattening the grass that stuck out like green spears from the tops of the mounds.

Fadfin then leaned heavily onto the stem and arched downwards, Thaddeus followed and saw how the ground was now approaching rapidly, Takt did the same and followed the pair, they were flying close to one another now as they dived, Fadfin kept on towards the ground and with each second they dived Thaddeus felt nervous that they would plummet into the ground but then Fadfin pulled hard on the stem as his whole body leaned backwards from the seed. Thaddeus copied instantly after and then so did Takt, they swooped low and were now travelling even quicker than they were when they were diving. The wind blasted past their faces as they gained on the valley and they swayed in the wind as the bases of the seeds lifted and twisted from left to right narrowly missing blades of grass and large flower petals that blurred past in colors of green, purple, blue and reds but Thaddeus concentrated more on flying. He held onto the stems firmly with both hands as they flew and as he looked over his shoulder at Takt he saw his clockwork companion smiling and laughing as they flew, Fadfin looked over his shoulder and was also laughing, his colorless eyes gleaming in the light. Thaddeus looked ahead and then let out a long cheer and laughed heavily as this was the most exciting experience in his life so far. The valley approached more quickly and was soon only moments away "Here we go" shouted Fadfin as he posed his body for quick maneuvers "Keep close my friends, keep your eyes on the ground as well and move if you see the rising warm air, we will soon be through so just hold on" He continued and as he said it they entered the valley, Thaddeus moved quickly and matched Fadfin's movements, they swung from left to right to not only avoid the hot air that Thaddeus instantly felt as they entered the valley but to also avoid the enormous branches which protruded from the thick mud below which looked like an endless sea of black sludge, not too dissimilar from what he and Takt had experienced in the Malimar.

They moved quickly and now Thaddeus was getting the hang of the movements of the dandelion seed, he moved of his own accord as he arched left and right, flying quickly over fallen branches and dodging the spearing petals of muddy looking weeds, the warm air pockets visible from the rising muddy vapor that looked liked the fumes that exited power plants in the world that Thaddeus remembered. He dodged them quickly and then became parallel with Fadfin, he looked over his shoulder and saw Takt flying close behind with a stern and concentrating look upon his face "We are nearly through my friends" shouted Fadfin and with that Thaddeus saw the end the of the valley, the light beyond becoming brighter and more welcoming, they hurried ahead until they were about to exit, but then a scream, Thaddeus turned quickly to see Takt being blasted high into the air by a muddy burst of air that escaped the thick mud below, Thaddeus shouted but didn't know what to do. He turned quickly to fly after his friend and used the remnants of the warm air to lift higher after Takt who now looked petrified and frozen with fear which Thaddeus had never seen in his clockwork companion. Thaddeus flew faster until he was nearly in reach, he pulled back on the stem and then leaned forwards, the weight giving him the boost he needed as he reached Takt and held out his hand. Thaddeus soon felt the cool metal from the clockwork fingers

grasp his hand and Thaddeus pulled his
friend closer until Takt grabbed hold of
the seed that Thaddeus was riding on,
Thaddeus uncoiled some of the stem and
tied it quickly around Takt's seed until
they were firmly connected but Thaddeus
didn't know what to do next and then, just
as he looked around for the aid of their
Fairy companion a small arrow came
spiraling through the air and pierced
through the two seed stems that Thaddeus
and Takt rode upon. The arrow had a thick
silvery rope attached to it that Thaddeus
soon realized was spider silk, they looked
ahead and saw Fadfin floating a few feet
away, he had fired the arrow from what
looked like a cross bow that he was
carrying but instead of being wooden or
metal, it was made from a black material
but Thaddeus had no time to think about
how Fadfin had helped and instead he and
Takt pulled hard on the spider silk, they
soon lowered in height and before long
were inches away from their Fairy friend
"Got to be careful with these places, you
never know when you're going to get
blasted into the air or eaten by a bird or
what not" said Fadfin, "Thank you for
saving us, how did you save us?" asked
Takt as they floated slowly away from the
valley, "With this" said Fadfin as he held
up an object that did resemble a cross bow
but was definitely made from something
peculiar as it seemed to have yellow
markings on it as well as black stripes,

"It's part of a wasp mandible, extremely useful for making tools with, the Pixies use them to ride into battle with, Draedan managed to kill a wasp many years ago, he cut the mandible down enough for me to use part of it as a sort of bow and arrow, the full mandible was much too big for me to use as a wasp is about twenty times the size of me" chuckled Fadfin as they floated further on "How far have we got to go?" asked Thaddeus "Not far, nearly there now" replied Fadfin as he pointed ahead to a hill in the short distance with a lonely tree sitting atop of it. They flew on for a short time before Fadfin started to lower his dandelion seed "We should set down now and continue at a larger size" the Fairy said with a slight chuckle to his voice, Thaddeus and Takt looked at each other with confused expressions on their faces but then soon followed Fadfin until they were passing through the grassy canopy. They set down onto the ground and disembarked their long stems, "Now, we are going to need to enlarge to the size the two of you were when you arrived at our world, we could not enlarge before the valley as the Moth Moss only allows the ability to shrink in our land, there have been times when one of us has needed to become larger and has accidently destroyed some of our village and ever since then the Moth Moss only allows transformations outside of the Fairy circle" said Fadfin as he handed Thaddeus and Takt a piece of the dark green moss, its smell was unusual and sweet but Thaddeus remembered the bitter taste it held. They all threw back the moss into their mouths and chewed quickly, all three of them keeping their eyes firmly closed, then, once the bitter taste had passed Thaddeus felt warm air blow down upon him, he then felt very dizzy as his legs became wobbly and unsteady. They rested his hand on a tree to steady himself and then realized, he was holding a tree and as opened his eyes he saw he was back to his normal size, he looked over at Takt and realized his friend was also now normal size and as he looked at Fadfin he saw the Fairy now standing as tall as they were, even slightly taller. Thaddeus thought it was quite odd to see their Fairy companion now standing at about six feet tall, his pale skin looking even more translucent, his wide but vacant looking eyes stared ahead of himself as he smiled "Well, that was rather fun, but shall we continue? The Trummelboot Hill is only moments away" and with that Fadfin turned and began to walk on towards their destination. Thaddeus and Takt began to jog after their Fairy friend who seemed to be able to walk faster now and with long strides, they saw the Fairy take out a long black robe from a bag he held around his shoulder just like Thaddeus with his satchel and belt that held his tools. The Fairy wrapped the robe around himself and pulled the large hood

over his round head. They had not been
walking long as they passed old and curled
trees, the bark now black with age and the
grass now clumpy and thick feeling under
foot, as they walked they came to what
seemed like a wall made from thick thorns
and branches "The Trummelboot Hill and the
Roterbaum Tree lay beyond this wall of
spikes, be careful as you pass through,
the thorns are sharp and the branches
thick which will make it hard to traverse"
said Fadfin and with that they began to
move forward into the barrier of large,
black spikes.

13.

A passage of thorns.

Each thorn seemed to snag on Thaddeus' clothes, and each thorn seemed to hook on the fabric that was wound around Takt, the only one who seemed to pass through the thorns with ease was Fadfin, he ducked and dodged each branch that held the long and sharp thorns which shone dully in the light that was seeping through the rooftop made from thorns. The travelers made their way slowly through the treacherous and giant hedge of thorns as the branches seemed to twist and bend on for eternity. Thaddeus felt scratches on his arms and hands and his feet hurt from stepping on fallen thorns below, he tried moving branches out of the way as he passed but they were heavy and firm in place, he resorted to ducking lower and stepping higher over the logs that formed the floor they walked upon. He glanced back at Takt who was slightly smaller than Thaddeus so found it a little easier to move amongst the thick thorn branches, Thaddeus looked ahead at Fadfin who moved so much easier than himself, he seemed to be passing though the terrain like smoke in the top of a tree, he was quick and nimble which made Thaddeus think of how much the Fairy

before him was part of nature and part of
the land, he could be what surrounded him
and move through it as if he were the
branches themselves. Suddenly Fadfin
stopped in his tracks and turned, he
looked back at Thaddeus and Takt who
stopped as well "We should rest here, we
shouldn't be moving at night, there isn't
far to go so we will exit the brambles at
first light" said Fadfin and with that he
sat on a lowered branch that had a small
gap in the brambles before him, Thaddeus
and Takt moved closer and sat on an
opposite branch which Thaddeus thought to
himself was surprisingly comfortable.
Fadfin leant forward and pulled out a
peculiar looking object from the small
satchel that was secured around the
Fairy's waist which Thaddeus noticed was
made from spider silk and seemed to hold
many different objects belonging to the
Fairy, the object which Fadfin held in his
long fingers was a deep green color and
looked like a folded leaf but then, the
Fairy squeezed the green object and a
spark of light ejected from it which then
floated down into a small pile of twigs
that Fadfin had kicked into place from the
surrounding area with his long and crooked
feet, the feet which seemed to blend in
with the ground and Thaddeus was certain
changed color depending on the color of
the surroundings, and as Thaddeus thought
he realized that all of the Fairy's skin
seemed to act like this, much like a

chameleon. The twigs suddenly sparked into a small fire that instantly warmed Thaddeus as the brambles around them had made the air very cool and with the sunlight soon fading it made Thaddeus all the more cooler so the fire was a welcome treat. Thaddeus warmed his hands and as he looked over to his clockwork friend he saw Takt making himself more comfortable by putting his feet up on an adjacent branch, the area surrounding their small campsite was now black with not a glimmer of light, not even from above which made Thaddeus feel a little uneasy but as he looked back at his traveling companions he felt the uneasy feeling soon vanish and as Fadfin revealed an unusual looking piece of fruit he soon returned to his familiar self "Well, today has been the most exciting day of my life I must say" said Thaddeus directing his comment to no one in particular, "It most certainly was" replied Takt as he put his mechanical arms behind his head an looked upward, "I felt alive, truly alive and I will never forget today" continued Takt as Fadfin looked up to the pair when he had finished slicing the fruit he had produced. It was green with a deep red centre and looked very tasty that Thaddeus could barely contain himself when the Fairy handed it to him, he eat instantly without missing a drop of the juice that ran from the fruit in his hands, it tasted much like that of a pear mixed with a strawberry, "That in your hands Thaddeus, is a Funnelwim fruit, it grows on trees we planted hundreds of years ago and every year it produces fruit that can fill a Fairy for at least five days but I do not know the effects on humans" and just as Fadfin had spoken Thaddeus immediately felt full and passed the rest of his fruit back to Fadfin who in turn looked over at Takt who was now smiling at the pair, "Will you not eat with us Takt?" Fadfin asked, "I do not eat but thank you, I never feel hungry or thirsty, nor am I supposed to feel tired" replied Takt, "But you are feeling certain feelings lately are you not?" asked Fadfin as he continued to look down at his fruit which was glowing a light green in the fire light. "I am" replied Takt after a moment, my clockwork body seems to be feeling certain things that I remember from being alive, such as muscle soreness as well as aches and pains, and more recently I have been having dreams which is unusual since I do not sleep but last night when we were back at the Dandelion House I slipped into my usual trance like state but soon after I actually slept and dreamt, it was a dream of beauty and of a land that was bright with color, much like the scenery we passed over before arriving here" said Takt, "Maybe it was Heaven you saw" said Thaddeus, "What is Heaven?" asked Fadfin with a slightly confused tone to his raspy voice, Thaddeus thought for a moment before speaking, "It is a place that some humans believe they will go to when they die, if they lead a good life they would go to Heaven, if they lead a bad life then they would go to Hell" said Thaddeus, "Ah, when Fairies die, we turn to a dust that feeds the earth, we are then reborn in the bud of a sunflower and then go on to live a new life, so do you believe in a Heaven Thaddeus?" asked Fadfin, "I'm not sure, I think I will believe it when I see it" replied Thaddeus, "Like the world you are venturing in now?" asked Fadfin with a smile on his round face, "Exactly, I had no idea that a world like this existed alongside my world without anyone ever really knowing, I like this world, I feel happy here, I feel happy to be traveling with the two of you" responded Thaddeus, "And I you" replied Fadfin as Takt moved forward he placed a hand on Thaddeus' shoulder, "And so do I" said Takt with a big smile upon his clockwork face that shone brightly in the firelight although his large pocket watch eyes still shone a bright green glow.

"I have a theory on your human feelings that are beginning to surface Takt, if you are interested in hearing it?" said Fadfin, "Definitely" replied Takt eagerly, "You are a Vormundgeist, and from what I know Vormundgeist's can possess an inanimate object, but after a prolonged period of time they seem to become quite attached to the object or what the object is doing, in your case your time spent with Thaddeus is actually passing human energy, alive energy onto you and thus making you feel the feelings he is experiencing but not only that, the feelings you are experiencing are actually becoming attached to you, so Takt Zifferblatt it would appear you are becoming more human the more time you spend with Thaddeus, which my friend is not a bad thing to happen, you still feel the power of the StarkStrom?" asked Fadfin, "Yes I do, I can still feel its energy within me" replied Takt, "That's good, it makes you a powerful Vormundgeist indeed" smiled Fadfin before returning to poking the flaming twigs that illuminated the area around them like a golden wall "That sounds very plausible" said Takt as he looked deep into the fire, "It is a form of protection" continued Fadfin "A pairing of two companions in order to protect one another, this is a good thing my friends as it will ensure that you both watch out for one another" and with that Takt smiled at the Fairy and also at Thaddeus who returned the smile but with a hint of confusion upon his face "Shall we get some sleep? I hope what I have said has shed some light on any of your concerns, but tomorrow will be a testing day so I suggest we rest now, I will put up something that will shield us from anything that dwells within the thorns and branches" said Fadfin before he stood, walked over to a large branch and climbed about six feet up the thorny branches. He took his spider web satchel and reached in, his arm seemed to reach in deeper than what the bag actually was but he then removed a thin sheet of some sorts and with it he looked back towards Thaddeus and Takt and threw his arms out overhead, the silky looking sheet floated high into the air and acted as a glowing cloud for a moment, it hung in the air between the thick thorns and branches before seemingly attaching itself to different parts of the surrounding brambles. It then began to slide down the branches but didn't lose any length and actually started to gain some as it sank lower until finally it touched the ground. Thaddeus looked around and saw that there was now a dome which surrounded them and acted as a large bubble that hung to the thorns and branches around them.

"What is that?" asked Thaddeus as he and Takt looked around in amazement, the heat from the fire had no effect on the protective film that encased them and in fact Thaddeus could still feel a slight breeze passing through "Spider web has many uses and not many people know that the silk from spiders has great magical properties" said Fadfin "This silk will allow us to be unseen while we rest, it is greatly used to protect our villages as well so we know it works well, sleep my friends as you will go undisturbed this night" and with that Fadfin jumped down and sat back on the same log he had occupied the entire evening and soon put his large Fairy feet up, rested his head on a small piece of moss and was soon breathing heavily. Thaddeus looked over at Takt "Good night Thaddeus" said Takt as he put his head back against his own piece of large branch and lay still, before long the glowing light from the pocket watch eyes dimmed, then went out entirely and with that Thaddeus turned towards the warm and glowing fire, stretched his feet along the ground and sunk off the branch before settling himself upon the soft ground, a ground that even with being surrounded by harsh and sharp spikes from cool branches was still as soft as freshly dug earth. Thaddeus settled in place and put his head back into a smooth groove of the branch behind him as he casted his eyes towards the crackling fire before him, he could feel the heat upon his face which made him even more tired than he already was, the aches and pains from the adventure of the day that was nearly at an end finally starting to catch up with him. He thought again at how his life was changing every moment that he continued on his adventure along with his good friend Takt and now another companion that was fast becoming just as good a friend, the Fairy Fadfin who was now breathing deeply across from

Thaddeus who finally closed his eyes and sighed deeply before falling fast asleep.

14.

Trummelboot Hill.

Thaddeus awoke lazily, his eyes were heavy
and his body felt instantly stiff from the
previous day's excursions. The scratches
he had acquired from scrambling through
the thorns still hurt and stung as he
probed the injuries, he sat up slowly and
looked around to see Takt sat opposite him
talking to Fadfin and as Thaddeus started
to stir the two of them looked across and
smiled, "Good morning there Thaddeus" said
Fadfin cheerfully, "Good morning" replied
Thaddeus in a croaky, early morning voice,
Takt walked over "Hello there, are you
ready for today?" he asked as he knelt
down next to Thaddeus "I think so, still a
bit sore from yesterday but I am ready"
said Thaddeus as he began to get to his
feet "Well Fadfin has just been saying we
are an hour at least away from exiting the
thorns, so please eat something and we
shall be on our way" said Takt as he
handed Thaddeus a piece of the fruit that
he had tasted the night before, but
Thaddeus declined as he was actually still
full from the piece of Funnelwim fruit, he
did however accept the small flask of
water that they had had since setting off
from the shop about three weeks earlier,

it was now full to the brim of crystal
clear and cool water which Thaddeus
thought was peculiar as it was near empty
the day before but as he looked over at
Fadfin the Fairy winked at him signaling
that he may have had something to do with
filling his flask. The water tasted smooth
and refreshing and seemed to give Thaddeus
a renewed sense of energy with which he
jumped up, fastened his trusty satchel
around his shoulder and which hung tightly
to his waist, he ruffled his hair and
looked at the other two travelers who,
when seeing Thaddeus's eagerness to set
off also stood and prepared themselves for
the day ahead. Fadfin removed the spider
web sheet that had hidden them during the
night, he then packed it away in the
spider web satchel before straightening
and looking over to Thaddeus and Takt,
"Shall we be on our way?" asked Takt and
with that Fadfin passed them and began to
lead them back into the thorny wilderness
that surrounded them. Before Thaddeus knew
it he was stepping back over large fallen
logs and dodging enormous spiked thorns,
he was more careful now as he did want the
injuries he sustained the day before added
to, they moved slowly but still Fadfin
moved with ease, he ducked and dodged like
he had done the day before but then
Thaddeus saw something he thought he would
never see, there was light ahead and the
light was approaching through the shadows
of the brambles around them, it gave

Thaddeus focus to move on and it made him push to get to the exit of this horrible place.

Twenty or so minutes had passed and the light that Thaddeus could see ahead was approaching now more rapidly and before Thaddeus, Takt and Fadfin could think they had come to the edge of the brambles, they stepped out onto bright green grass and as the sun shone brightly onto the three travelers faces they all felt a sense of relief, and also happiness to finally be out of the dark and cold bramble bush. Thaddeus looked around at the land that surrounded them as Fadfin sat down on the soft grass and felt how full of life it was and how it seemed to vibrate with goodness, unlike the ground that they rested on the night before which felt dead and lifeless with which nothing could live within. Thaddeus gazed around and saw that the grass stretched on for a short distance unlike the bramble bush that stretched to the left and right of Thaddeus for miles and miles, the grassy land led to a hill which was unusual looking in the bright sunlight that seemed to almost silhouette it in the early morning sun. It was lumpy with bulbous areas protruding from it and sat atop it was a lone tree that stretched into the sky like a crooked hand, Takt came to Thaddeus' side "That is the Roterbaum Tree and the…." "The Trummelboot Hill" Fadfin interrupted as he came to Thaddeus' left side "We must be quick as our presence will most certainly attract the Pixies, so please let us continue and finish our task" and with that Fadfin began to lead again, they walked quickly across the open land all the while gazing around for any signs of danger, the air was quiet and the land still as they progressed past lone trees that seemed to be smaller than the Roterbaum Tree, there were boulders which were covered in moss and looked ancient and also slightly like the Dollgrat Stones which Bolgreena Mollhog drew her power from. They moved on and were fast approaching the Trummelboot hill and before long they stood only a few feet from the area in which they had to ascend, the hill rose in front of them which left the three travelers in shadow with its size, "Be wary here my friends as the Pixies dwell in the Roterbaum tree atop this hill, we must be quick and get the Moak Crone Pearl from within the trunk of the tree, I know that the Pixies will be aware of our presence and will try to attack but if we can get back to the thorns we can surely lose them as they fear those brambles for reasons I do not know, so let us proceed" said Fadfin, Thaddeus and Takt did not speak as they understood the words of the Fairy, they began to move closer to the incline in the ground and were soon clambering on hands and knees to reach the top. The hill was

unusual as the grass was thin with areas
missing to reveal the hard and grey earth
below, the earth was rough with areas that
looked stony but the stones did not move
which allowed the three companions area to
grab in order to get a better climb. They
kept moving and were soon reaching the top
of the first ridge and when Thaddeus
looked back he saw that they had climbed
well over thirty feet and still had quite
a climb to go. They kept climbing but this
time much more smoothly as the ground was
easier to ascend, it was ridged and bumped
like crumpled paper and allowed them to
climb to the peak of the second ridge
which when completed allowed Thaddeus and
Takt to get a good view of the tree they
were trying to get to. It stood only a few
feet above them and with the sight of it
they set off eagerly to conquer the
Trummelboot hill. Another few minutes had
passed and finally Thaddeus, Takt and
Fadfin had reached the top, they stood and
looked around briefly at the landscape
around them which was beautiful, it was
bright with green colors that glowed from
the grassy land and made Thaddeus think
about the holiday he and Pandora had taken
to Yorkshire a year before her death, it
was peaceful here which Thaddeus liked but
he did not have long to dwell on these
thoughts as there was a task that needed
to be completed.

"Remember my friends, be careful and wary" said Fadfin as they stood looking at the large Roterbaum Tree before them, its branches were red as well as its thick trunk that was covered in a glowing green moss, its leaves were a deep green and hung from the long and thin branches which stretched high into the sky above. It was an impressive sight Thaddeus thought to himself but there was something… else about the tree, there was something evil that emitted from it in some unknown way that made Thaddeus feel uneasy and as he looked over at Takt he saw in the clockwork face that his friend and companion felt the same feelings but they needed to do this and with that Thaddeus made the first tentative step towards their goal. Takt followed closely and then Fadfin and as they approached the tree they noticed something, no Pixies had shown themselves and they still didn't as they came right up to the trees trunk with the moss hanging in front of them with its green glow and bitter smell "Moth Moss?" asked Thaddeus "Yes, we have our own source that grows within the village so we do not need any for now but what we need is within the tree" and with that the Fairy reached forward and began to feel the moss for any breaks in it that would lead to an opening. Thaddeus did the same and so did Takt and soon all three of them were feeling the soft moss but before long Thaddeus' hand went further into the tree

"I think I have found it" Thaddeus said in a loud whisper in order not to draw attention, he looked upward into the canopy of leaves and branches above and saw no movement as Takt and Fadfin approached from either side of the trunk "Reach in Thaddeus, you should be able to feel the Moak Crone in easy reach, the moss protects it but once you reach into the tree you should be able to just take it" said Fadfin, Thaddeus reached deep into the tree which was cool inside with a damp feel to it, it felt as though mist was trapped inside and like he had just put his hand into a hole that contained winter fog. He felt around until his fingertips passed over a cool object that felt smooth to the touch with angular edges that were sharp like that of an uncut diamond. Thaddeus grasped it and pulled, the pearl came away with his movements and he was soon drawing it from the tree trunk, in the sunlight Thaddeus held the Moak Crone Pearl, it was a deep blue which resembled that of Takt's StarkStrom power, it looked as though it would burst into bolts of lightning at any moment as Thaddeus was sure he could see movement within the pearl, a swirling of colors if anything but Thaddeus was wondering more about the weight of the large stone as he had imagined it to be heavy with its overall size but instead it was very light, as though he was holding a pebble. He looked up at Fadfin who was smiling at him "Well done Thaddeus, please let me have it and I shall keep it safe" said the Fairy with which Thaddeus handed over the Moak Crone Pearl and saw Fadfin quickly put it into the mysterious spider web satchel about his hip. "We must go now" said Fadfin who began to turn but then Thaddeus heard a sound, he couldn't really tell what the sound was but it was definitely coming from up in the trees branches, it sounded almost like a hum, like the buzz of many bees but then he saw the look on Fadfin's face, it was that of horror and fear and just at that moment there was a mist that sprung from the top of the Roterbaum Tree which swirled in the air and began to descend towards them "Pixies!!" shouted Fadfin who instantly began to run, Thaddeus and Takt darted after the Fairy and were soon running at a sprint. Takt's clockwork legs were running so fast that he seemed to overtake Thaddeus, they reached the point in the hill in which they had ascended before and all three of them felt an unusual moving sensation. They hurried down the side of the hill and partly tumbled to the first bulbous ledge and started to run along it adjacent to the steep part of the hill that they had just tumbled down. Then, the hill moved, it moved so much that Thaddeus, Takt and Fadfin were all knocked off their feet as the ledge they were stood upon rose into the air, the mounds on the hill rolled and moved, they shuddered which made dirt and rock fall with incredible force. Thaddeus and the two companions got to their feet and ran towards the lowest part of the hill, they got to the edge and saw what looked like a giant hand rise from the dirt as Trummelboot hill continued to thrash and move, "It's a Troll! The hill is the Troll, we need to jump or we will die here" shouted Fadfin and with that he grabbed Thaddeus and Takt and pulled them as he jumped, the three of them flew through the air for what Thaddeus thought was an incredibly long time before finally crashing into the long green grass which Thaddeus was thankful for instead of stone or any other hard surface. They did not look back but instead ran for the cover of the large black thorn forest that they were once afraid of but now longed for its protection. They ran for their lives as the sound of the massive Troll raged behind them along with the humming and buzzing of the flying Pixies, they did not stop until a huge boulder flew over their heads and into the giant thorn hedge, it crashed through the branches and spikes with incredible force, crumbling what stood in its rolling way with ease "That is our passage, we must go, come quickly my friends" Fadfin shouted as they continued to run and before long they had reached the entrance to the long thorns. Thaddeus turned as they entered and saw a glimpse of the Troll, the sun was still on

the rise behind it which only allowed
Thaddeus to see a giant silhouette which
seemed to blot out the sun, its arms were
nearly as long as its body which were
pressed against the ground, its legs were
enormous and thick like huge tree trunks
and its head was quite small in comparison
to the rest of its body but its torso was
wide and bulky seemingly made of stone and
dirt like the earth it had risen from.
There was a misty haze that was moving
towards them along now with the Troll that
was stepping one massive foot ahead of the
other and was moving towards them,
Thaddeus turned and hurried after his
friends to try and get to safety. They ran
not caring that the sharp spikes kept
piercing them as they passed, Fadfin still
seemed to move with ease through the
branches and thorns but was still hurrying
greatly as Takt and Thaddeus hurried
behind, they had been running, ducking and
dodging for what seemed to be a long while
and decided to sit and rest for a moment
to catch their breath but it wasn't long
before they could all hear a crashing
noise before the dreaded hum of the swarm
of Pixies. They moved on quickly but as
Thaddeus and Takt glanced back they could
see the Troll moving through the branches
and with its huge arms it broke and
crashed through each part of the brambles
that were in its way and from what
Thaddeus could see the Pixies were
gathered around the Troll seemingly

sweeping the air, "They are looking for us" Takt whispered and with that they moved on quickly.

They stepped carefully with Fadfin, their foot falls were soft in order not to crack the broken and dead branches that lay at their feet, they stepped over logs slowly and tentatively as they moved, "Where do you think they are?" asked Takt, "I'm not sure, I cannot hear the sound of the troll anymore" said Fadfin as they moved, "Be quiet!" said Thaddeus suddenly, and with that all three of them dropped to the ground and lay still, just a moment after Thaddeus had signaled his companions there were loud thuds which quickly grew closer along with the crunching and cracking of the large thorn branches around them. Fadfin reached into his spider web satchel which lay at his side and pulled out the thin sheet which hid the travelers from view the night before, he quickly covered the three them and lay still, to Thaddeus he didn't feel any different only that there was something very light that rested upon him which did not take his fear away as a foot of the large troll came into view. Thaddeus saw that the large mud encrusted foot was grotesque with its warty texture and through the mud Thaddeus could see its grey color like that of a large boulder which rolled and twitched as it moved. The foot crashed through the large brambles as it swung forward and

then a hand came crashing through before
resting on the hard ground, Thaddeus saw
the thick fingers with moss sprouting from
around the large black fingernails,
Thaddeus looked upwards without moving too
much and saw the tree in which they had
taken the Moak Crone Pearl from was now
protruding from the back of the large
troll, it pointed out like a giant spear,
its leaves and branches swaying and
bending as the troll moved from side to
side as it swung its round head and thick
neck in search of the three travelers. A
faint mist that moved in different
directions to the cool breeze now hovered
around the troll's head as it shuffled
clumsily forward and Thaddeus knew that
the mist was actually the swarm of Pixies,
"They will not be able to see us or sense
us, just do not make a sound" said Fadfin
quietly who was lying flat next to
Thaddeus and Takt who was remaining still
and silent lay to the right of Thaddeus.

The three lay for a long while as the
troll searched the area but thankfully not
as thoroughly as Thaddeus thought it
might, it slowly started to move away
crushing the brambles with its massive
feet as it went, the mist of Pixies now
blending into the black branches as they
moved with the troll into the shadowy
beyond. Thaddeus, Takt and Fadfin lay
still for a while longer, the sound of the
troll disappearing into the distance but

after a few minutes had passed Fadfin pulled back the spider web covering and stood, Thaddeus stood also and dusted himself off before Takt got to his feet, "Do you think it has gone?" asked Takt Zifferblatt, "I don't think so, it will still be searching the thorny brambles along with the Pixies" said Thaddeus as Fadfin rounded on them, "We must move! and quickly!" but with that the Fairy knelt on one knee, placed his long fingers on the ground and closed his large colorless eyes, a humming could be heard coming from the Fairy which sounded more like distant thunder but much quieter, but a moment later the Fairy stood and began to move ahead using the gap in the thorns that the troll had made to ease their passage, "What did you do just now?" asked Thaddeus, "I summoned our way of traveling back to the Dandelion House" said Fadfin as he looked over his shoulder with a slight smile upon his face, "Our way of travel?" asked Takt with a slightly confused, "You will have to wait and see my friends but our main concern right now is to get to the edge of this bramble forest" said Fadfin and with that the three of them moved on with haste. The journey was easier than before as the destruction to the thorny forest that the troll had caused made it considerably easier to navigate through, they stepped over fallen branches and crushed thorns and before they even knew it they were exiting the bramble forest. Thaddeus breathed a sigh of relief and so did the other two travelers as they all expected the troll to come crashing through the branches at any moment of their journey. "Quickly friends, this way" said Fadfin as he walked on through the more pleasant part of the land, the grass was green again and the trees curled but seemed full of life if not very old and tired. They moved on quickly as all three of the now tired travelers kept looking over their shoulders and into the trees that were lined on each side of them but then, to Thaddeus' relief he saw ahead a small rise in the ground not two feet in height, the grass swayed atop the small mound that ran from left to right into the trees and had a small gap in it that created a slight V-shape. Past the bump in the path was a wide open field that stretched on with a pleasant mist which hung close to the ground and in the distance Thaddeus could see the silhouette of a large tree, it was the tree that stretched high above the Dandelion House and Fairy village below and Thaddeus knew that this part of the journey was finally over.

Fadfin stopped and reached into the spider silk satchel, he pulled out three small portions of Moth Moss and handed a piece to Thaddeus and a piece to Takt but then, just as Thaddeus was about to chew on the bitter moss there came a rumbling a

crashing sound from with the thorn forest.
It got louder and louder and then the
troll appeared, it came smashing through
the thorns which partly stuck into the
thick and muddied skin. Thaddeus got a
good look at the troll and saw how hideous
it appeared but it did look like part of
the earth around them, it had vines and
grassy patches that hung from its torso,
its hands were like rocks just like its
over-sized feet, its head was also rock
like but with two large and pointed ears
that aimed downwards and were slightly
green in color. It's body had lines that
looked like small trails leading all over
it from the years of lying still and
becoming the actual Trummelboot Hill, its
eyes were large and a light green with a
long slit for a mouth in which small
yellowing teeth protruded upwards and also
downwards at all angles. Thaddeus didn't
have too long to look upon it as Fadfin
forced the moss into he and Takt's mouth
and urged them to chew before pulling them
at a run towards the green rise in the
earth "Hurry, we must go!" The Fairy
shouted as they ran, "The troll cannot
cross the Fairy circle but the Pixies can,
we must not let them see which way we go!"
Thaddeus could barely hear what the Fairy
was saying over the thumping and pounding
of the troll's heavy body in pursuit; it
was gaining quickly on them and just as
its large hand was swooping towards them
Fadfin pulled them all into a jump, their

bodies flew through the air and at that
point the world suddenly got much larger,
the hand of the troll started to shadow
them from sunlight as they seemed to fall,
the ground got further away as Thaddeus'
insides suddenly lurched and twisted as
they fell. He could see the trees and
plants start to tower over the three like
massive skyscrapers as they fell, the Moth
Moss was taking effect and soon had them
at a rapid fall towards the ground and
towards the valley in which they had flown
through on dandelion seeds the day before.

"Take my hand!" shouted Fadfin as they fell and Thaddeus grabbed it almost instantly before Takt grabbed Thaddeus' right hand tightly, and just then Thaddeus saw three white balls floating below them but which were getting larger by the second, it was the dandelion seeds but they seemed to be being flown by someone else but then Thaddeus saw as they got closer that they were being navigated by three Fairies, and as Thaddeus, Takt and Fadfin were almost upon them a string of spider web was spun around their waists and were suddenly pulled towards the Fairies and the floating transportation. Thaddeus was attached to the middle dandelion seed and as soon being hauled upon the wide bottom which hung below the bright white parachute. A tall Fairy stood with him with a wide smile on his face, "Glad you could drop by" The Fairy said with a high pitched and slightly child like voice before laughing heartily, "Thanks for the rescue" said Thaddeus who was out of breath from the excursion, he looked over and saw Takt being pulled onto a seed by a female Fairy before he saw the clockwork eyes glance over and cast a wave in his direction. Thaddeus waved back before seeing Fadfin float overhead with a small looking Fairy steering his dandelion seed, "We must get back to the village before the Pixies know which direction we have gone, it will not take them long" shouted Fadfin before swooping off through

the dark valley and before long Thaddeus
and Takt were in pursuit, quickly darting
up and above then down below the half
sunken logs, the pilot of his dandelion
was much more experienced than he was when
they had begun the journey for the Moak
Crone Pearl and seemed to have no fear of
this dark place but before long the now
six travelers were exiting the valley and
swooping extremely quickly amongst the
blades of grass and beneath the mist that
hung above them, it's now large droplets
of moisture occasionally sliding down the
grass nearby or suddenly dropping from the
mist clouds above.

Thaddeus looked back and when his gaze
passed Takt he saw his clockwork friend
was doing the same, but their vision was
impaired by the thick fog above, Thaddeus
was glad of this as he did not want to see
the now even larger troll standing there,
its large eyes peering for them but to no
avail. The Fairies, human and clockwork
traveler had escaped the troll's grasp,
but had they escaped the Pixies?

15.

A welcome return.

The dandelion seeds floated downwards
gently after what seemed like long hours
of traveling, Thaddeus had sat down on the
comfortable dandelion seed base, his legs
swung freely in the breeze as the moved
and as he looked over at Fadfin he saw the
Fairy that had helped them stay alive was
fast asleep on the base of the seed,
Thaddeus looked for Takt who he saw
floated a few feet above them and who was
peering down with a smile on his clockwork
face, his arm extended ahead in a pointing
motion and with that Thaddeus looked ahead
but as he looked ahead he heard a faint
noise with which he couldn't identify
right away, but as they floated forward he
started to recognize the sound. The
village came into view as the large tree
began to shadow them with the sun started
to sink deeper into the land, the haze
from the mist surrounded the returning
travelers and what welcomed them were
cheers and claps from the Fairies that
stood atop the dandelion flowers. The huts
that were concealed within the fluffy
white heads were aglow with the lights
within, Fairies stood on the bridges which
were lined with the small glowing orbs

that Thaddeus was so fond of. Thaddeus, Takt and their companions sunk deeper into Fairy village passing crooked bridges that were strung between the dandelion plants, they sunk past huts that were crooked and inviting and were soon landing upon the large green leaf to the welcome of Draedan the large black spider, this time though Thaddeus was not afraid and was actually pleased to see the large arachnid which showed as the travelers disembarked the dandelion seeds and ran towards the spider as his booming voice greeted them, "It is good to see you dear Thaddeus and Takt, I am so pleased to see your safe return but please continue up to the Dandelion House, Feen Lowenzahn is excited to see you" and as Thaddeus and Takt looked back towards Fadfin they saw him talking with the Fairies that had rescued them before he turned and waved them on with a nod and a smile. Thaddeus and Takt almost ran up the steps that wound up within the stem of the large flower which held the Dandelion House atop it. They soon exited through the hatch in the floor of the small nest like room before heading down the corridor towards the large entrance of the house of Fairies which was now filled with Fairies of all shapes and sizes, the Fairies who were once wary and nervous looking now couldn't be more different. The Fairies cheered and clapped before coming forward to shake hands and hug the returned travelers, the thin frames which seemed almost see-through were friendly and Thaddeus couldn't be more pleased to see them all. Their wide eyes which were absent of pupils or color but still seemed welcoming stared in amazement at their return, the Fairies guided Thaddeus and Takt up the stairs towards the chamber of Feen Lowenzahn, they seemed to jump the stairs two at a time as they ascended and were soon upon the large wooden doors, they pushed and heard the creak of the vines that acted as hinges and were soon entering the chamber of Feen Lowenzahn who stood at the dragonfly window with a wide smile upon his round face.

"Come closer my friends, tell me your tale" said the Fairy king with his booming voice echoing through the large room, and with that the three of them moved towards the large table made of bark and sat, Thaddeus then began to tell Feen Lowenzahn the adventure they had just returned from, all the while Feen kept a smile on his face with his eyes fixed upon Thaddeus, Takt interjected at times and described what had happened when they had encountered the large troll of the Trummelboot Hill with which Feen looked suddenly interested, "So you saw the Troll?" asked Feen, "Yes, we saw it when we were stood upon it after we had taken the Moak Crone Pearl, and when we had jumped from it, it chased us while the Pixies hovered around its head" said Takt with his voice raising as he recalled the moments of the adventure, "So the Troll was the hill?" asked Feen, "Yes, it had the Roterbaum Tree growing from its back" said Thaddeus, "Fascinating, I have heard about the trolls hiding within the landscape, there are some on the coast of Wales, they appear to humans as the sand dunes on the beaches even though they do not grow as large as the Troll you encountered, other Trolls disguise themselves as trees or bridges as well" said Feen but with the king's last statement Thaddeus was reminded of something he had heard or even felt when they were within the Maug Lake, the bridge they crossed before meeting Bolgreena seemed to Thaddeus to move, it also seemed to be rumbling in some way, Thaddeus thought that maybe the bridge was another Troll that had been awoken by his and Takt's passage, but the booming of Feen Lowenzahn's voice brought Thaddeus around again and out of the daydream he was within, "You did well my friends" Feen said, "You found the Moak Crone Pearl, something that will protect us and keep us hidden, and I am a man of my word" With that Feen beckoned to another Fairy with his long hand, the Fairy briefly exited the room before returning with Fadfin a few steps behind, the Fairy they had traveled with was carrying a very ornate box with which he placed on the bark table in front of Feen, winked at both Thaddeus and Takt before stepping back behind the Fairy King who was now opening the black box.

Feen Lowenzahn reached his long fingers into the box and pulled out what Thaddeus and Takt had wanted to see for so long, it was another piece to the Todesfall Clock, Feen paused with the piece in his hands for a moment and looked at the two companions who were staring at the piece of clock, "You must wait until you have acquired all three pieces before putting them together, be careful with this my friends and guard it with your life, I hear that the Malimar servants are growing stronger the longer they are in this world, but as long as they do not possess all the pieces then we are safe, but the last piece you seek resides with two of the Malimars most evil creations, the Ink Twins, they are foul in nature and are made from the very ooze that runs within the Malimar world. They seek the other two pieces and that you are taking the two pieces right to them will make your journey extremely dangerous but as long as you remember your Obsidian Glasses Thaddeus, they will allow you to see the clock piece and also the evil of the Ink Twins, and as long as you use your StarkStrom Takt then I believe in the both of you" said Feen Lowenzahn before handing the second piece of Todesfall Clock over the Thaddeus who stared at it, taking in its magic before looking up at Takt and then sliding it into the satchel that rested at his hip.

"But for now, please rest, rest as long as you like here and enjoy our village for as long as you need, but I must go I have business regarding the Moak Crone Pearl to attend" and with that Feen Lowenzahn stood and began exiting the room before stopping and looking back over his tall shoulder, his branch like horns standing tall from the round head before saying "It is good to see you, all three of you" and as he rested a large hand on Fadfin's shoulder he exited.

"Can you remember the rooms you stayed in previously?" asked Fadfin, "Oh yes, it is easy to get around once you have been here" said Thaddeus cheerfully and with that Fadfin exited through the same door that Feen Lowenzahn had gone through which left Thaddeus and Takt standing in the large room alone for a moment, "It seems as though this journey may get quite dangerous after we leave here" said Takt, "It does seem that way, but the way I see it is that we have just escaped a stomping from a giant troll, we outrun and escaped from the swarm of Pixies that threaten the Fairies, we have already traveled to the Malimar, fought the Jewel Box Dolls and won, confronted Bolgreena Mollhog and won her over so after all that I feel as though we can do anything and we will beat the Ink Twins. We are in this together and we will be in this together until the very end and I am glad we are doing this with one another" said Thaddeus as he placed a hand on the shoulder of his clockwork friend, "I feel the same, if we weren't able to complete our adventure then we wouldn't have gotten very far now would we?" said Takt, "Exactly! Now let's go and rest, I want to sample some more Fairy food" said Thaddeus and with that they exited the large room and headed for the rooms in which they stayed in two nights previously.

They rested well, the beds being a welcome change from the cold floor they had slept on the night before, with thorns, dead leaves and hard branches sharing the ground with them they now felt relaxed with the warm rooms and welcoming atmosphere. The small glowing orbs that lit the hallways and long walkway outside of Thaddeus and Takt's room which looked down upon the Fairy village and which looked out upon the dandelions with the small Fairy huts lodged within them, the bridges and walkways lining the stems and flowers ahead which glowed in the now dimming light. Thaddeus felt happy with the nerves of the next stage of their journey fading away slightly as the silence surrounded him, he felt as though he could stay here forever but he knew that resting himself was the most important thing right now, he needed to be prepared for the confrontation that awaited them.

Thaddeus and Takt stayed within the Fairy village for the next two days, Thaddeus sampled much of the food the village had to offer whilst Takt met many of the Fairies that lived in the area, they were friendly and inviting as some invited Takt and Thaddeus to stay for dinner with their families. On the first full day Thaddeus managed to visit Draedan who was busy harvesting more dandelion seeds for the Fairy travelers that would soon be leaving to visit relatives at nearby Fairy villages but the second day in which Thaddeus and Takt had agreed to be on their way was soon upon them. They were stood out upon the large flower in which the Dandelion House stood upon when something seemed different in the air, nor Thaddeus or Takt could identify what felt different but it made them feel uneasy and as they looked around they realized that the same feeling that lurked within them had spread throughout the village as many Fairies stood around looking uncomfortable but then, Thaddeus heard something, he couldn't tell what it was but it was gradually getting louder, it now sounded like a humming which was coming from somewhere within the dandelion forest that surrounded them. The humming seemed familiar but as Thaddeus realized where he had heard the unusual sound before Pixies came swarming through the large dandelion stems, instantly Fairies began to run in all directions as the crooked looking creatures came jumping down from the plants above. More and more came funneling through the stems and leapt down into the village where they pounced upon Fairies that hadn't reacted as quickly as some of the others, Thaddeus saw Fairies being torn limb from limb as Pixies darted in and out of the huts, they looked like Fairies but were now much more hunched over, scars and tribal designs were strewn upon their dark grey bodies, their eyes were like Fairies as they were void of pupils or any color at all and they looked dead unlike the Fairies that were full of life, these hideous creatures oozed evil and were much more primitive than their humanoid relatives.

Already Fairy blood was splattered across the ground below as the Pixies swarmed through the village like ravenous monsters; they came from the sky with their wings seemingly made from dead feathers but fear soon released Thaddeus for a moment as he turned to run to grab Takt and Feen he saw Fairies coming behind him. They were running in formation with what seemed to be armor attached to their torsos which under closer inspection was actually walnuts, the Fairies were wearing

Walnut armor and branded in their long
hands were what seemed to be long spikes,
they ran forward and started to stab and
spear the approaching Pixies which showed
how well trained in combat the Fairies
were, they ducked and dodged the long and
clawed hands of the Pixies and drove the
glistening spikes deep into the skinny
bodies of the Pixies.

Thaddeus turned to grab Takt before
running back towards Feen who was now
stood facing the Pixies, a long spear of
his own held tightly in his long fingers,
"You must go my friends" the Fairy king
shouted, "We will not leave you here, we
want to help" shouted Thaddeus, "Give us a
weapon" shouted Takt and with that the
tall king ran with them to a passageway
between the Dandelion House and the small
hut that was stood next door. They ran
before coming to a small decline in the
flower which lead to a fallen twig, past
the twig lay a long piece of bark that was
roofed by what seemed to be a long red
petal from an unknown flower, attached to
the bark were large nettle leaves that had
the long glistening spikes protruding from
them, "Nettle stings" said Thaddeus, "Yes,
they prove quite effective against the
Pixies as they hold a poison that
paralyses before killing them, be careful
with them" said Feen as he stepped back
and produced the walnut armor from another
part of the bark wall, Thaddeus and Takt

pulled a spike that had a small green patch at its base which acted as a good handle, it felt weighty in Thaddeus' hand much like a sword with its length being about the same. They quickly attached the armor and ran back towards the battle which was now starting to overrun the flower that held the Dandelion House upon it. Feen suddenly ran forward, he spiked and stabbed the Pixies as they came with incredible speed, he leapt over three at a time and stabbed them deep into their backs, he kicked and threw Pixies that became to close huge numbers of feet away and started to clear an area around himself.

Thaddeus and Takt ran forward and started swinging their nettle sting swords at the nearest Pixies, the heat of battle soon took over the pair as they started to slay Pixies in all directions. Pixie blood soon covered their hands and sprayed their faces as the fought hard against the Fairy enemy, the hoard was increasing and before Thaddeus knew he was stood alone in a group of Pixies that advanced on him, he ran at them and slammed his body hard into a group of the hideous monsters.

He felt their hot steamy breath against his face, their grotesque teeth were spiked and sharp against his forehead, they felt slimy and cold and absent of any life as he pushed against them and as

Thaddeus pushed he was grateful at how light they were, he continued to push and was soon at the edge of the flower, with a final push he heaved the Pixies over the edge of the flower and watched them plummet to a messy death in the village below. Thaddeus stood breathing hard for a moment before scanning his vision back towards the Dandelion House looking for his companion, just as he searched he saw a bright lightening blue light shine from the middle of a group of Pixies. Takt's StarkStrom was taking over and as Thaddeus ran towards his friend the bolts of the StarkStrom ejected from the centre of the group and instantly killed the Pixies surrounding Takt. as Thaddeus got to Takt, Feen Lowenzahn ran to them and pushed them hard towards the Dandelion House, "You must go, the village is lost, you must go and finish your quest" shouted Feen Lowenzahn, "We won't leave you" shouted Thaddeus as he speared an approaching Pixie, "You must Thaddeus, you must survive and finish your quest, if you stay here you will die now go!!" shouted Feen, "I have a feeling we will see each other again my friends, now go!!" and with that the tall Fairy king turned and charged a group of savage Pixies that were stood waiting for the tall Fairy, strings of drool falling from their open mouths, their eyes staring wildly at their enemy as they all stood hunched together in one dark mass.

Thaddeus and Takt turned but saw something they had not expected, it was Draedan now covered in glistened armor that seemed to be made from a form of metal, the large spider charged the Pixies and speared them with his many spiked legs, "Go my friends, I have covered you so get in the house and get to the Dandelion seeds!" said Draedan with his raspy and wind-like voice, but with that the sound of crashing came, it was a house across from the large Dandelion House and it was crumbling to the ground, Pixies overrun it as some were even crushed under the wood that came tumbling down. Thaddeus and Takt ran through the Dandelion House and soon came to the hatch in the ground that led to where they had left off for the Trummelboot Hill a few days previously, but as they entered the hatch Takt felt a boney hand on his shoulder, it was Fadfin who was now armored in the walnut, "Feen requested me to accompany you, well we ordered me to protect you so I am coming along" said the Fairy who stood stooped above them half in the passageway, not a word was said as they all understood what needed to be done and with that they all hurried down the narrow passage within the dandelion stem. "Continue down to the last leaf" said Fadfin as they descended, it did not take long to reach it and as they exited the small doorway that was carved into the stem they saw hundreds of dandelion seeds lined before them on a slightly browning and curled leaf that sat still some height off the ground below, but Thaddeus did not have long to dwell on the sight before him as Fadfin ran forward and untied three of the seeds, "Quickly we must leave" he said with a hint of haste in his whispered voice, the three boarded their seeds and like before, kicked off hard with one foot and were soon floating upwards and to the south of the Dandelion House. The sound of crashing wood and screams from both Fairy and Pixie spilled into the air but soon faded as they escaped, and before long all was quiet again and Thaddeus began to dwell on the Pixie attack and whether or not any Fairies would survive it.

16.

A familiar face

Thaddeus, Takt and Fadfin floated upon
their dandelion seeds for what seemed like
hours, none of them spoke and instead they
just gave each other occasional somber
looks. The grief that was holding them all
felt unbearable as they felt so helpless
and knew they couldn't go back to try and
help the Fairies as the number of Pixies
was too great. The journey seemed endless
as they floated but then Fadfin broke the
silence "Don't let your hearts hang heavy
my friends, my people have a way of
finding their way out of trouble, the
Pixies must have followed us as we
returned to the village" the Fairy said,
"Your village has been destroyed Fadfin"
said Thaddeus, "Ah the surface part of the
village has, but there is more to our
world than meets the eye, we have tunnels
and a whole village underground, each
dandelion that the bridges connect to and
which the huts sit atop all have
passageways leading down through the
stems, much like we traveled down to get
our seeds and when we met Draedan, they
all lead deep underground to a place we
built many centuries ago and which is
impenetrable to anything other than

Fairies, yes many Fairies may have died in the attack but many will have fled instantly into the passages and waited for the attack to be over, once the Pixies leave the Fairies would surface, place the Moak Crone Pearl into its stone and begin to rebuild our village" said Fadin, "What about Feen? Do you think he is alive?" asked Takt, "Our king is strong and has made his way out of much worse situations than the attack of the Pixies" said Fadfin, "Our destination is approaching, we must start our descent" said the Fairy before suddenly standing and then leaning on his dandelion seed which slowly started to move downwards, Thaddeus and Takt did the same and before long the three companions set down on the ground which was shadowed by large overhanging blades of grass. The dandelions were now gone and had been replaced by tall grass that had large weeds towering into the sky above.

Fadfin took out three small pieces of Moth Moss and handed two of them to Takt and Thaddeus, "We cannot continue at this size" said Fadfin before placing the Moss in his mouth and began to chew, not wanting the Fairy to suddenly become a giant Thaddeus and Takt quickly began to chew on the moss and within a few moments the ground around them shot away at incredible speed. The leaves that once towered around them were now far below and they found themselves stood in a small patch of grass that was surrounded by small dense trees. Fadfin pulled a black cloak from within his spider web satchel that seemed to be endless in its interior as Fadfin often brought out objects from within it that looked far too big to carry in such a small bag. The Fairy wrapped himself in the cloak and pulled the hood up around his head to partly conceal himself, "Let us go" said Fadfin as he lead Thaddeus and Takt through the trees that made the air feel cool and reminded Thaddeus of the bramble forest they had camped in on the way to find the Moak Crone Pearl.

"Do you know where to go?" asked Thaddeus, "We are on our way to visit someone you may recognize" said Fadfin as they moved through the small wood but before long they stepped out from the line of trees. Thaddeus looked around and saw that they stood upon a road which made Thaddeus think about the life he had come from. The road in front of them had been made for humans and maybe there would be a car which would suddenly pass them, it made Thaddeus feel strange as he remembered his human life and how far away from it he felt. The three travelers stood at the edge of the grey road and looked out upon a vast golden field of corn, Thaddeus and Takt quickly looked at one another, "Manni Mais" they both said in unison but as they looked at Fadfin they saw the cloaked

Fairy looking back them, smiling as he crossed the road before standing in front of the large and towering hedge that separated them from the corn field, Fadfin then steped into it, disappearing before their eyes. Thaddeus and Takt eagerly crossed the road as the sun peered over the woodland behind them and warmed the back of their necks. They stood before the hedge, looked at each other and stepped into it, they felt the branches of the hedge seem to bend away from them as they walked which lasted only a moment and suddenly the two travelers found themselves stood within the cornfield. Tall golden branches of the corn they remember so well from their first meeting with the Man of the Corn stood high above them as Fadfin stood smiling at them, "Come quickly, Manni Mais is waiting for us" said the Fairy as he quickly moved on, leading Thaddeus and Takt on and as they pushed through the thick stalks they came to a small clearing, stood there, as crouched over as the pair remember was Manni Mais who still wore the same clothing and still wore the same welcoming expression as he had all those weeks ago. The basket of snails that Thaddeus remembered being the small Sidhee's was held tightly in his grasp, "Hello my friends" said the Man of the Corn in the welcoming and very crispy sounding voice he possessed.

"I wondered when I might see you two again and you have brought a friend?" asked the Man of the Corn, "My name is Fadfin, I am from the Fairy world" said Fadfin as he stepped forward and removed the hood that shrouded his face, "Ah, it has been many centuries since I met one of your kind, it is good to meet you Fadfin" said Manni Mais as he stepped forward holding his hand out ready to take the Fairies grasp, Fadfin responded by firmly gripping the small man's hand and shaking, Manni looked over at the other two travelers and smiled, "You look like warriors" he chuckled and at that moment Thaddeus realized they were still wearing the walnut armor with the nettle sting sword fastened at their waists, "I guess we do" said Takt as he laughed quietly. "I knew you would be back, but the question is why have you returned?" asked Manni Mais, "We require to travel somewhere" said Fadfin as he spoke very vaguely, and with that Manni Mais stepped back and gazed at the three of them, "You are searching for the last piece of the Todesfall Clock are you not? Or do you already know where it rests?" asked the Man of the Corn as Fadfin stepped forward, "We need to find the Ink Twins, they hold the last piece of the clock" and as the Fairy mentioned the evil names, Manni Mais' face changed to more of a grimace, "Do you know where they are?" asked Fadin, "Yes, the Twins dwell within the towers, the towers are surrounded by the pollution that the twins give off, it is a place with a black sky and a toxic land that surrounds it" said Manni Mais, "I can allow you to pass to the land but you must take care, the land there only possesses death and decay, the door will take you to the edge of the land and once you pass it you will be on your own" and with that the Man of the Corn rested his basket of snail fairies on the ground and stepped towards the three travelers, the familiar humming sound emitted from the small corn man and soon after the Sidhee's started to flutter from the basket. The corn began to bend with the humming and vibrating and soon the sight of a door made from corn stems could be visible as more stems creaked into place. Thaddeus looked on in amazement and still could not believe how impressive the sight before them actually was, but before long the door stood six feet in front of them as the Sidhee's fluttered back down to the ground and lay still. Manni Mais stepped forward and placed his small crooked hand onto the corn door, it creaked open and allowed Thaddeus, Takt and Fadfin to look through it, the sky around where they stood was bright blue with warm air swirling around them but through the corn door the sky had turned a dark red color, there was a smell that oozed through the door which smelt of fumes and sewage. Manni Mais looked back at the three companions and beckoned them to pass through, Fadfin moved forward and as he passed through he turned and nodded briefly at Manni Mais, next was Takt who walked forward to meet with a reassuring smile from the Man of the Corn before passing through into the gloomy land, next was Thaddeus who walked forward with which he was met with a hand on his shoulder, "Be careful my friend, and remember that your Obsidian Glasses will allow you to see in the darkest places, keep them close and watch out for one another, goodbye my friend" said Manni, "Good bye" said Thaddeus and with that he walked through the door into the polluted air.

Thaddeus turned nearly immediately after stepping through the corn doorway to see the tall stems that had made the door already creaking and braking to nothing, the Man of the Corn was gone and they stood in the gloom alone, the three travelers looked on through the field of corn that was now decaying in the polluted air, through the broken stems, past the brown and dead hedge that bordered the field around them and through the leafless trees. Upon a rise in the earth stood a black shape against the deep red sky, two black towers protruded from it and seemed to pierce the sky above as thick plumes of black smoke bellowed out of the towers, the smoke filled the air and made its way into the nostrils of Thaddeus and Fadfin and even though Takt could not smell he

still held a grimacing look upon his face
as he took in the sight around him into
his glowing green pocket watch eyes, "We
must move forward" said Thaddeus as he
took the first steps towards the
foreboding towers, towards the last piece
of the Todesfall Clock and towards the Ink
Twins.

17.

The Ink Twins.

The three travelers moved through the now
dead corn field and soon came to the
equally dead looking hedge that bordered
the field. Fadfin moved forward and
stepped close to the hedge but as he moved
forward to pass through he snagged his
cloak, his skin was pricked by the thorns
which made him push through the tough
hedge instead of easily passing through
which was what had happened in the
previous field they had visited. Soon all
three companions were safely through the
hedge, they stood upon a dirty track that
may have once been a road but now looked
like a dark orange sandy trail and the
dust seemed to constantly linger in the
air, it made breathing difficult as
Thaddeus' chest felt tight and his breath
raspy. Fadfin looked on and saw the large
black building wasn't far ahead, "We are
not far and we must keep moving, the Twins
dwell in the building over the tree line"
said Fadfin as he moved on, Thaddeus and
Takt ran to keep up, their feelings were
more numb than Thaddeus had expected, the
thought of finding the last piece of the
clock spurred him on and the fact that
their journey was coming to its end made

him all the more eager to move. Thaddeus
moved on as he felt his shoes tearing
underfoot, the sharp rocks and stones
pierced the base of his foot with each
step, he looked at Fadfin's feet and saw
they were bloody from the hard ground as
well. Thaddeus looked around as they
briskly walked and saw a land of dead
things, he had no idea where they actually
were but he did not like the sight that
seemed to close on him inch by inch, it
felt overpowering with its stench and also
with its dark smoke that lingered around
every corner. The ground seemed to grow
darker and where there was once grass now
lay pools of black slime that poured from
large round pipes which stuck out from the
sides of the now black mounds of earth.
They moved on following the dead tree
line, the small branches that curled above
their heads like demon hands, like boney
hands which were reaching for their lives
to take into the black land around them.
As they rounded a corner in the now muddy
track they passed through a small gap in
between two large hills with which the
tops were hidden in a black mist. It
didn't take long for them to pass through
and once they exited the small valley they
were confronted by a sight which none of
them would ever forget, before them stood
the massive black structure with its two
black towers which looked like two large
and evil fingers that pointed to the sky
above, scaffolding hung closely to the

corners of the building and looked almost like a skeleton. It was an evil place as the feeling they all got from it was that of death and bad things. Thaddeus swallowed hard and moved forward to the structure that he thought looked like a big factory as its smoke pumped from the towers to meet with the already heavily polluted air, the sky above cracked with thunder that made Thaddeus, Takt and Fadfin jump out of their skin and fabric. There was no lightening and Thaddeus thought that the lightening had been hidden by the deep red sky that was thick with toxic moisture which hung close to the towers.

No words were spoken but Thaddeus heard the footsteps of his trusted friend Takt close behind and also the gentle tapping from the large feet of the Fairy Fadfin close behind his clockwork companion. They moved downwards and came ever closer to the thing they all were dreading and before long they were passing over a steel bridge that hung low over a black river, a river that bubbled and popped with a thick sludge that gave off a hot mist which instantly made Thaddeus feel uncomfortable and sick, it made all three of the travelers pass over the bridge quickly and as they crossed they were confronted by a large metal door, although the door was wide open something made Thaddeus stop in his tracks as though a wall was in front

of him but hidden from view. Fadfin came
to his left and Takt to his right, they
all looked forward into the back opening
before them, "We must enter" said Fadfin,
"There is evil in this place" said Takt
but Thaddeus held back his fear and
stepped forward but as he passed through
the large open door he suddenly felt
chilled as though all life had been taken
from the room. Fadfin came next but was
just a slightly red silhouette as the red
light filtered through behind him but also
passed through his almost see-through
body. Takt entered last and looked around
warily at each corner of the large room
they now stood within, his glowing green
eyes shining brightly in the darkness. The
room had large metal walkways that lined
the ceiling, they dripped with black ooze
that the travelers were careful not to
have any drip onto them, they quickly made
their way through the empty room that
still felt as though it was occupied by
hundreds of watching eyes, "We are being
watched" said Fadfin as he walked close to
Thaddeus and Takt, "I do not know what by
but we are being watched by something" he
continued, "It is more than one thing"
said Takt, "There are many creatures here,
I fear they are Ooze Slaves from the
Malimar, we must keep going" Takt
Zifferblatt continued and with that the
three hurried into the next room, it was
much larger than the first but just as
empty, the room's ceiling was layered with

a thick black smoke that hung high above them.

There was a churning and grinding noise coming from far below that sounded like the grinding of a large metal mechanism, they hurried through the room but soon found themselves in its very center. "They are here" whispered Takt as he suddenly stopped, "We must fight them" said Fadfin as he stood back to back with Thaddeus and Takt, his large eyes gazing in all directions to see where the Ink Twins lurked but then they heard the Twin's voice, "It is about time you arrived here Thaddeus and Takt, but you have brought a friend we see" said the voice that seemed to come from all directions, the voice sounding like a bubbling hiss, much like a snake that could speak under water, it was a grotesque sounding voice and with each word there seemed to be the dropping of thick blobs of ooze coming from up above. Thaddeus looked up before shouting "How do you know our names?" he roared confidently, "We know lots about you, our friend the Domovoy saw you at the train station on the first day of your travels, he notified us of your intentions and ever since we have eagerly awaited your arrival" the dribbling and hissing voice said as Thaddeus heard a giggling coming from the dark corner ahead of them, Thaddeus and Takt squinted to see what was making the noise, "What is it?" asked

Fadfin as the tall fairy twisted his head over his shoulder but Thaddeus had no time to respond as he saw whatever was in the corner come skulking forward, it was the Domovoy, the bearded and homeless looking man stepped out of the darkness briefly, his gloved hands with the fingertips removed held over his grubby looking mouth as he laughed, Thaddeus and Takt were filled with dread as they saw the dark creature before them, it kept laughing before "Be Quiet You Fool!!!!" shouted the evil voice from above and with that the Domovoy slipped back into the shadow and was quiet once more, "Who are you?" shouted Thaddeus even though he could have guessed the response, "We are the Ink Twins, we have lived here for an age and we are the rulers of the Malimar" said the Ink Twins and with that the sound of dripping above grew louder and then the three companions saw the ooze that slimed from above until large pools of the black slime grew on the dark grey floor. The ooze moved towards them before it suddenly rose, out of the black blob in front of them formed two large shapes, they separated and soon took the form of two figures, they stood tall above Thaddeus, Takt and Fadfin and had long black arms that dripped the ooze around them but as the slime touched the ground it reattached itself with the rest of the black ooze. Their bodies were glistened black like thick oil and then Thaddeus saw their faces which were near identical, they had white eyes which glistened in the dim light, the white of the eyes was a vast contrast to the rest of the setting around them but the eyes held no life they only held death and evil, and so did the gaping mouth the Twins possessed. They had sliming teeth that were made of the same grotesque ooze that the bodies were formed of, the mouths slimed open into grins that showed Thaddeus and Takt a glimpse of the deep green coloring within the hideous maws, "You were foolish for coming here, we will kill all of you and take the clock pieces" the Twins said as they grinned down on them, a long arm protruded from the black mass of the twin on the left, its fingers were dripping with the slime as its fingertip stroked the side of Thaddeus' face, "So full of life, it will feel so good to take that away" said the hissing voice with its devil like grin.

Thaddeus' mind flashed back to his wife, his deceased wife that he had loved and still loved with all his heart, her face flashed before his eyes and gave him the urge he needed, it gave him the feeling and push to fight as he would not die here he would not die at the hands of these evil creatures and with that he grasped the nettle sting sword at his waist, Fadfin seemed to notice his companions movements and moved his long fairy fingers over the hilt of his own nettle sting

sword. Thaddeus breathed deep with his
eyes closed, he breathed in, and out
before pulling the sword from his waist
and lunging forward into the oozing
beasts, he drew the sword back and drove
it deep into the black ink that seeped
over his hands but the Ink Twins struck
Thaddeus and he soon felt himself flying
back through the air before striking into
a hard object and slumping to the ground.
He shook his head to regain stability as
he stood and as he looked up he saw the
Ink Twins holding Fadfin by the throat and
seemed to be choking the Fairy, "Hey!!"
shouted Thaddeus as he got to his feet, he
briefly looked to his side and saw Takt
standing next to him looking a little
beaten and scraped before he looked back
at the oozing mass before them, "Let him
go!!" screamed Thaddeus in a voice he
barely recognized and with that the Ink
Twins turned to look at Thaddeus and Takt
before letting out a hideous roar that
screeched through the air, pieces of black
slime spattering through the air with the
noise.

Thaddeus instantly began to run forward,
his legs feeling alien as he ran and he
saw he was quickly approaching the dark
giants before him, out of the corner of
his eyes he saw more dark masses moving in
to aid their masters but then a bright
blue light like bolts of electric came
spurting past him, they struck into the

dark shapes and Thaddeus saw the Domovoy get struck from his feet. It was Takt with his StarkStrom who was now stood upon a large metal frame and was firing the lightening power from his clockwork fingertips, the bolts of the lightening flew in all directions and with each bolt it found a target whether it be the Domovoy or another oozing creature that slimed out of the shadows. Thaddeus moved quickly forward until he leapt into the air, he buried the nettle sting sword deep in the neck area of one of the Ink Twins, he fell to the ground again before stabbing at the body area of the inky monsters, Fadfin was dropped next to him, the Fairy quickly stood before grasping at his own sword that lay on the ground nearby but as he stood he saw a hideous creature approaching, it had a black body but long spikes that stuck out in all different directions from its crooked back, its face had large white eyes that gazed at Thaddeus and Fadfin blankly, the blue light from Takt reflected in its dead expression, it roared and charged Fadfin who held the nettle sting sword before his body. He charged and was soon stabbing at the creature as its claws ripped at the Fairy, but Fadfin was too quick and within moments he had leapt behind the creature, jabbed the sword deep into its spine with which the monster instantly let out a terrible howl, its mouth opened wide to show its completely white inside, the teeth glowed in the dark room and before long it dropped limply to the ground, its legs twitching with the large spike like sword jammed into its back. Fadfin pulled the sword out and ran to Thaddeus' aid and as he moved he killed hideous creatures with swift strikes. The creatures ranged in size but all had the grotesque and slimy look to them, some did not have eyes but smelt the air to search out prey, some had arms that were longer than their bodies and allowed them to move with incredible speed but none were a match for the Fairy as he spiked and stabbed into the faces and bodies of the Malimar servants. Before long the Fairy joined Thaddeus and both started to stab at the Ink Twins who moved like thick water around them, but now Takt was running to help his friends, he shot the StarkStrom at creatures that still approached from the darkness but soon, he joined Thaddeus and Fadfin and began firing the StarkStrom at the oozing creatures and with each blast of bright lightening the creature recoiled, they were in pain Thaddeus thought to himself, but they fought harder and occasionally turned to stab at the creatures of the Malimar that tried to attack from behind but they did not succeed in taking the three companions by surprise and soon lay dead in the dim light. The dark floor soon began to feel slippery with the oozing blood and slime that flowed from the skin and innards of the dark creatures that now lay slumped around them.

Thaddeus, Takt and Fadfin were now stood on all sides of the Ink Twins and were stabbing at the thick mass before them, occasionally dodging the swiping arms that tried to strike them, the ooze and slime splattered across Thaddeus's face as an arm swooped over his head as he ducked, he stabbed upwards and ripped at the arm that now felt as though it had some substance within it, the Ink Twin howled in agony as it lost one of its arms. Thaddeus threw it far into the room's corner so it could not re-connect with its master, he stabbed more at the creature but as he became more confident he stepped closer to the slimy creature and in an instant one of the oozing arms struck down upon his head which made Thaddeus feel dizzy and nauseous as he fell to one knee. Fadfin and Takt saw their companion fall and ran to his aid, still slashing and stabbing at the creature that was now slowing with its missing limbs and pierced body, the two ran to Thaddeus and helped him up but just as Thaddeus got to his feet he felt Fadfin's grasp tighten and as Thaddues looked into the eyes of his friend he saw something different looking back at him, there was no longer an absence of color but now a faint glow of light green around the edges, Thaddeus looked down and saw an inky claw protruding from the belly of

Fadfin, it was oozing with the black slime from its claw tip before exiting the body of the Fairy, Fadfin felt limp and fell to one knee, "Fadfin?" asked Thaddeus, "Fadfin no!" his voice now shaking as his friend fell to the floor, Takt looked stunned but his StarkStrom lit brightly from his clockwork hands and in an instant shot from the pointed and metal fingertips into the slimy bodies of the Ink Twins that now seemed to be merged together to make one large creature, with each bolt of StarkStrom the large inky mass moved back against the wall of the black room, "Get Fadfin to the corner of the room!!" shouted Takt "I'll hold it off!" he shouted and fired more electric light at the monster. Thaddeus pulled his friend along the floor until they reached the corner of the room; the Fairy's eyes now a soft green color, "Fadfin, you're going to be ok" said Thaddeus as his voice trembled more and more, "Just don't you go anywhere" he said but as he said it, Fadfin's long fingers rested atop the hand of Thaddeus, they felt cold to the touch and seemed a more browner color than they had before, Thaddeus looked at his friend through teary eyes, "I am so glad I got to meet a human" said Fadfin with a croaky voice, "You are so brave Thaddeus, I will never forget you and it was such a pleasure to let you see my world, I hope you liked it" said Fadfin with his final breath, "Fadfin?" said Thaddeus but there was no response and as Thaddeus looked down at the Fairy's motionless body he felt the skin of Fadfin become harder, he then seemed to break apart but Thaddeus soon realized that he was crumbling into leaves, there were different types of leaves from many different types of trees that scattered across the ground, and soon the entire body of Fadfin had crumbled to hundreds of leaves that then lifted into the air and gave the room a sign of life for a moment before dispersing into a faint mist that soon disappeared.

Thaddeus looked up at the fight between Takt and the Ink Twins and saw the light blue electric striking the body of the evil creature. Each strike cast enormous shadows across the walls of the now screeching beast, Thaddeus reached into his satchel and pulled the Obsidian glasses from deep within it, he placed them over his eyes and allowed them to rest upon his nose and ears, he gazed through the black lenses and golden curls that edged the lenses and spiraled to their centre, he looked at the Ink Twins and saw a glowing shape emitting from its centre, he looked harder and realized it was the final piece of the Todesfall Clock, the final piece was hidden within their inky, foul bodies and now Thaddeus knew what he had to do.

He stood and straightened with the nettle sting sword held tightly in his grasp, he stepped his foot forward and then the next until he was at a run but then, Takt was struck hard across his fabric and clockwork body, he flew through the air and crashed hard into Thaddeus, the metal arms of Takt crashed into Thaddeus' face which smashed the Obsidian Glasses that crumbled to the ground as the pair slumped together. Takt sat up quickly and looked toward the Ink Twins who were sliming against the walls in the corner and were not approaching yet. Takt pulled Thaddeus up, "The last piece of the clock is within the Twins, I don't know how to get it though" said Thaddeus as he climbed to his feet, "I know a way" said Takt as he kept his gaze on the oozing monsters, "I need to use the StarkStrom, I need to use the complete power of the Strom and I will need to use it from the inside, we must jump into the bodies and as you grab the clock piece I will use the StarkStrom to destroy the Ink Twins who will lose most of their power that holds them here on Earth once the piece of Todesfall Clock has been taken by yourself, and with the blast of blue lightening they will be sent back to the Malimar for good" said Takt, "OK then, let's do it" said Thaddeus eagerly but as he turned and started towards the hideous and oozing creatures Takt placed a metal hand which was smothered in black ooze on Thaddeus' shoulder , "Wait my friend, there is something else" said Takt with a hint of somberness in his voice, "The power I will use to defeat the Ink Twins will take my soul from this body and force me to pass over and I will not be able to return" said Takt as Thaddeus stared at him, "So doing this will kill you?" asked Thaddeus, "But you can't die" he continued with his voice now starting to crack, "You are right Thaddeus, I cannot die but my soul can be moved on, the body I possess now, the body you created will become empty once again but with that the Ink Twins will be defeated and you will possess all three pieces of the Todesfall Clock, we must do this Thaddeus" said Takt, "But we have been through so much, you are my best friend, what am I supposed to do without you?" asked Thaddeus with his eyes filling with tears, "I will always be here Thaddeus and I will always watch over you, you are my best friend as well and I feel honored to have journeyed with you, and I trust we will meet again one day but please Thaddeus let us defeat this monster, your life will be so much better after this my friend, I promise" said Takt Zifferblatt with a smile across his clockwork and fabric face which was now dirtied with black ooze and dust from the dark factory room they stood in. They looked at each other for a long moment before Thaddeus understood; he turned to face the Ink Twins who were now split in

two again and advancing towards the two
companions. Takt stood at Thaddeus' side,
"Together until the end my friend" he said
with a smile and the pair started to run
towards the creatures, tears streamed down
the face of Thaddeus before he leapt with
a roar, the nettle sting sword
outstretched in front of him as he jumped
forward and as Takt jumped forward the Ink
Twins screamed in a rush and the four
collided. Thaddeus sunk deep into the inky
bodies of the Twins as did Takt and
instantly Thaddeus felt the slime around
him become hot but it did not burn him, as
it got hotter he felt in his empty
outstretched hand the feel of an angular
shape, it was the last piece of the clock
and with that Thaddeus grasped it tightly,
dropping his nettle sword to become lost
in the ooze, he held it with both hands
and did not let go.

Through his tightly closed eyes he could
see a blue light, it was shining and
dancing through the ooze and was making
Thaddeus' face warm with its energy, he
could feel the presence of Takt next to
him but just as he was about to reach out
for his friend there was a massive bolt of
lightning that sparked all around him. The
ink seemed to become loose as the blue
light exploded and then Thaddeus felt the
presence of Takt next to him disappear,
and all of a sudden Thaddeus felt himself
drop, he fell for what seemed like a long

moment before colliding with the hard ground and as he kept his eyes tightly closed he could feel the ooze drop around him but it no longer had a form and instead felt like large blobs of paint falling all around him.

He opened his eyes and saw the thick pools of black ink lying all around him; it covered his face and matted his hair. The thick blobs covered his hands but as he gazed at his right hand he saw a glistening object that was free of the black ooze, it shone at him with its shiny black surface but it also had a shining red jewel at its centre as well as a clock hand that protruded from the right hand side.

Thaddeus saw the clock hand was ornate and silver but had no scratches or even a smudge of dirt upon it, it was the last piece of the Todesfall Clock, "Takt, we did it" said Thaddeus in a croaky voice, "It's over, we have defeated the Ink Twins and closed the Malimar" he continued but with no answer or response, "Takt?" Thaddeus said again as he rolled over to look for his friend, but then he saw, he saw the lifeless body of Takt Zifferblatt lying on its side, the once glowing green pocket watch eyes were now dull, the cogs and mechanisms that once ticked and spun were now quiet and unmoving. Thaddeus got to his feet and dashed over to his friend, he crouched next to his companion and looked with one hand placed on Takt's arm, "Takt?, Takt? Please wake up" said Thaddeus now crying, "I can't do this without you, together until the end remember?" he said as he looked upwards towards the dark ceiling of the factory, but what he soon realized was that was in fact the end, Takt had been with him from the start and had not left his side, his body was Thaddeus' creation and he had been glad of the company once they had set out on their adventure, they had kept each other safe but more importantly Takt Zifferblatt had been a friend, just like Fadfin had, they had shown Thaddeus his true self and how to be strong and unafraid, but now Takt was gone and so was Fadfin and he was alone again.

18.

A Fairies work.

Thaddeus lay next to Takt for a long
while, tears streamed down his face freely
and onto the cold floor as he still held
the last piece of the Todesfall Clock
tightly in his hands but soon something
urged him to move. He pulled himself up
and stood for a moment listening to the
silence that surrounded him, the ink had
gone and so had the creatures and now the
factory looked much different even though
it still looked dark and depressing, it
now had a different feel as though all the
bad things had been drained away and all
that was left was the structure. Thaddeus
leant down and picked up the empty body of
Takt Zifferblatt, he began to walk from
the factory with the clockwork doll held
in his arms.

The walk was a haze to Thaddeus and as he
stepped into the light he felt momentarily
blinded, the shapes that surrounded him
were not clear but seemed much brighter as
the sky now seemed blue and not deep red
with the thick pollution. He kept on
walking with his numb legs, all of his
body felt numb as he walked in no real
direction, he looked to the sky and down

at Takt again in the hope that his best
friend would have somehow magically came
back to life, but he was wrong, the body
of Takt still lay lifeless in his arms
that were blackened from the ink they had
both fought against. Thaddeus did not know
in which direction to travel, when the
three companions had traveled towards the
factory the land all looked the same but
now everything was very different and
didn't seem to be the place he had
traveled through a few hours before, or
maybe it was that he did not really care
about his direction of travel. He kept
walking but every few steps he stumbled
due to fatigue; he stepped onto a road
that seemed to be made from gravel and
dust before falling through some form of
brambles. He moved forward but suddenly he
felt a hand on his shoulder, his eyes were
still blurred and his feelings were filled
with grief that made him not care of the
stranger that was stood near him. There
were no words from the figure stood near
him but Thaddeus could hear fluttering and
the sound of branches twisting and
cracking. Before long the figure pushed
Thaddeus forward slightly before saying
gently "Well done my friend, and don't be
too solemn, you will see your friends
again one day" and with that the voice and
figure was gone, Thaddues walked forward,
he moved forward for a long while as fresh
tears streamed down his face but before
long he sensed a change in the land around

him, the ground became soft and the air breezy which seemed cheerful with a sense of life floating around him. He stood still as he felt the breeze around him change and with the new breeze he blinked to clear his eyes from the dust and tears, his vision soon cleared and he saw a white mist begin to encircle him. He then saw it was not a mist but it was dandelion seeds floating all around him, they swirled and danced around his body that was a stark contrast to the green and blue landscape around him, he was covered in the staining ink and his face was blackened with dirt. The seeds and gossamer spun wildly around him, it lifted his arms and passed through his fingers, his hair was blown and lifted as the seeds brushed past him; his clothes began to bend and crease and before Thaddeus knew, he was being lifted into the air with his feet floating at about six foot off the ground, the mist of seeds became denser and harder to see through, but as Thaddeus was gazing around he felt the piece of clock leave his hand, he tried to reach after it but failed and then the other two pieces left his satchel and joined the third piece in mid air. Thaddeus saw the clock pieces begin to rotate in the air and then saw that it was the dandelion seeds and gossamer that were holding the objects or more so the Fairies that flew the seeds. The clock pieces began to fit together and each cog and mechanism slotted together with ease in the white mist that surrounded them.

Before long the clock had been fitted together and with the last mechanism being slotted into place with the jewel at its centre that had been previously split into three pieces was now one, it glowed brightly suddenly and sent swirls of red, green and blue light spinning into the air around him. The color surrounded him and seemed to make the fog of Fairies turn the colors that were being emitted, Thaddeus looked on not knowing what was happening but before he knew it the empty body of Takt had been lifted from his grasp and gently put upon the ground. Thaddeus looked ahead into the swirl of Fairy travelers and suddenly saw a figure begin to emerge from the white, it seemed as though the person was simply walking through the air but without any features apparent but before long the person stood before Thaddeus who could see him more clearly now, the person was a young man with sleeked back blond hair that was hard to identify as the figure seemed a more see-through white. He was a young man maybe in his mid-twenties, he had a slim and slender face with pale eyes and who was also wearing a white shirt and waist coat, "Hello Thaddeus, it is good to see you again" the man said in a very familiar voice, "Who are you?" asked Thaddeus, the man's bright reflection visible in

Thaddeus' still watery eyes, "Don't you recognize my voice? It's me, Takt" said the man with which his last statement left Thaddeus stunned as he floated within the Fairy cloud, "Takt? I thought your soul… you died, did you…?" stuttered Thaddeus with which Takt gave a wide smile that seemed similar to when he had smiled in the clockwork body, "My soul passed over, I exited the clockwork body when I used up all of the StarkStrom, but my soul was not destroyed, but Thaddeus you must listen, you did it! You beat the Ink Twins and saved the world from the Malimar's cruelty, you are a hero" said Takt still keeping the wide smile, "I could not have done it without you Takt" said Thaddeus as his voice again became croaky, "And I could not have summoned the StarkStrom without you, you gave me a reason to fight the twins and for that I thank you Thaddeus, and do not worry as I will always watch over you my friend but I must be going" said Takt, "Please don't go!" said Thaddeus at a near shout and with an outreached hand, "Don't worry Thaddeus" another voice said that Thaddeus did not recognize, and then another man appeared stood behind Takt, he was tall and skinny with a slim black moustache that lined the edge of his top lip, he held his hands tightly behind his back and stood up straight, "You have done something that many of us thought was impossible, you stood against the Mailmar rulers and won,

well done Mr. Loveguard, you are a hero"
he said as the pair turned and began to
walk away, "Wait, who are you?" said
Thaddeus urgently, "I am Gideon Lilleyman
and it is a great pleasure to meet you
Thaddeus" and with that they started to
disappear and Thaddeus heard Takt call
back "Good bye Thaddeus, we will meet
again one day" and with that they were
gone, but Thaddeus felt a presence stood
behind him and as he spun in the air he
saw the figure of Fadfin stood there, but
now he had large branch like horns much
like Feen Lowenzahn but Fadfin now had a
glow about him. The Fairy did not say
anything but instead bowed and smiled, he
then began to walk past Thaddeus and
towards where Gideon and Takt had walked
to, the air then seemed empty for a moment
but as Thaddeus looked around he saw
another figure walking towards him, this
figure seemed different and then Thaddeus
realized who it was. It was his Pandora
and as she approached, Thaddeus felt
himself cry at the sight of her beauty, of
her long curled brown hair, her small nose
and bright blue eyes. She came close to
him and held his hands but even though
Thaddeus could not physically feel her
grasp, the sight of her hands upon his was
good enough and he felt a large smile
break across his face, "Hello my Thaddeus"
she said, "It is so good to see you" "It
is good to see you Pandora, I have missed
you so much" said Thaddeus, "I have missed

you too my love, but I have been watching as you journeyed on your adventure, I am so proud of you and I am so happy to see you fight for something" said Pandora as she placed one of her small hands upon his face, "I fought so that I could see you one last time" said Thaddeus as a tear fell from his face, "Well, you won Thaddeus and you have saved so many people from the evil that was coming into this world, you have made me so happy" said Pandora, "Please stay" said Thaddeus, "I cannot my love, I have to go now, but remember that I will always love you and I will always be watching over you, you are my soul mate and nothing will keep us apart" said Pandora as she leaned forward and gently kissed Thaddeus before stepping backwards, smiling and beginning to walk towards Fadfin, Takt and Gideon.

Thaddeus cried but it was a happy cry, he had seen his beloved Pandora and his best friends once more and they were OK, they were in another place now and one day he may even see them again, but as Thaddeus looked on the figure began to become white and cloud like before slowly ascending to the clouds above and were then one with the sky. Thaddeus looked upwards for a long while and did not notice the Fairies dispersing and setting him down on the ground, he knelt and felt the green grass under his dirty hands and as he looked down at the soft grass, he smiled but when

he looked up to notice the Fairies who
were now floating away, he saw one
dandelion seed floating a few inches from
his eyes, Thaddeus could see a faint green
glow who he knew to be Feen Lowenzahn, the
Fairy King and once the king had joined
the rest of the cloud of Fairies to travel
to wherever they dwelled now, Thaddeus got
to his feet, looked about the land he was
in and started on the long journey home.

19.

Home.

Thaddeus traveled for many days before he reached a train station, he had carried the empty body of Takt Zifferblatt for many miles and he now felt sick with exhaustion. He bordered the small train and rested his head against the seat as the train jolted forward. Takt was slumped next to him which made Thaddeus think back about the start of their journey and at how Takt was dressed in a long coat to hide what he looked like, the memory made Thaddeus smile as the train shot past green countryside that made Thaddeus wonder what fantastical creatures dwelled past the window, was their trolls lurking in the woodland in the distance? or were there Goblins or even more Witches out there somewhere? Thaddeus closed his eyes for a only a moment but within seconds he was fast asleep and dreaming of his bed on the second floor of Pandora's Box Of Clox shop down Giggleswick Street. He felt as though he had only been a sleep for a moment before he felt a hand shake him awake, he awoke with a start to the sight of an old lady, a lady he recognized from somewhere, "It's you" the eccentric looking lady said in an accent that brought it all back, it was the lady who had sold him the clock pieces and old broken doll at the car boot sale all those months ago, "Oh, Hi, I didn't recognize you for a moment" said Thaddeus sleepily, "Me neither, and I must say you don't half look rough, what have you been up to?" she said sounding slightly concerned, "You wouldn't believe me if I told you" said Thaddeus under his breath, "Is that the doll I sold you?" she said as she pointed to the lifeless body of Takt Zifferblatt sitting in the seat next to Thaddeus, "Urm, yes it is" said Thaddeus as he tried to conceal his friend, "It looks good, I might have to buy it off you" she said as she reached into her bag, "No! I mean, it's not for sale" said Thaddeus firmly, "Alright I was only asking, but you best get yourself together, we are almost at Grimpo Grotton so have a good day and I will pop into your shop at some point, my clock is playing up, see you" she said as she walked away and with her last comment Thaddeus felt something he had not felt in the months he had been away, it was a feeling of normality.

The train eventually stopped at the Grimpo Grotton station and Thaddeus made his way through the quiet station, he glanced over at the bench in which he remembered the Domovoy staring and laughing at them from and even though the Domovoy was now banished back to the Malimar he still felt uneasy walking past. Thaddeus carried the clockwork doll back through the streets until he found himself walking down Giggleswick Street. He felt strange for only a moment and then a familiar feeling overcome him that made him feel as though he had never left with which he hurried down the quiet street and before long he was stood in front of the Box of Clox shop. He quickly got the keys out of the satchel he had held with him for the entire adventure and inserted them into the lock which turned with ease. He stepped into the shop and looked around for a moment, nothing had changed, no more dust had settled on the crooked shelves, the shop still looked dim with the blinds drawn and not a sound could be heard.

Thaddeus locked the door behind him and walked through the shop, he placed the clockwork body that had once been possessed by Takt onto the seat behind the counter and made his way up the creaky stairs, before long he stood at the foot of the crooked bed in the dark and dusty room and fell onto it with a audible creak and groan that exited Thaddeus' slightly open mouth, but soon Thaddeus' snoring could be heard as he fell fast asleep.

Thaddeus awoke with a start as the surrounding room seemed strange from the places he and Takt had slept in over the last months, but after a moment the room

became familiar with its crooked walls and
dark paint, the dark red curtains still
hung as they did when he had left for the
incredible journey that was now over. He
sat up and stretched, looked at the clock
and realized that he had been asleep for
over twelve hours, but he did feel better
for it and as he stepped out of bed he
felt a sense of rejuvenation and decided
to go downstairs to open up the shop.

But first he decided he needed to clean
himself up, so he went to the shower and
spent the next thirty minutes scrubbing
off the ink and dirt that had encrusted
itself onto his skin, but when that thirty
minutes had passed Thaddeus Loveguard felt
like a new man and with his hair brushed
for the first time in years and his shirt
now ironed with a clean tie, and with his
jeans freshly washed he wandered down the
creaky stairs and into the shop. But
before he opened up he decided he needed
to have a bit of a spring clean, he got
out a new duster from the downstairs
kitchen and spent the next two hours
cleaning the shelves, floor and windows of
Pandora's Box of Clox, the dust was thick
and Thaddeus made his way through four new
dust clothes and two mops before he was
done. When he was done the shop looked
magnificent and like new, the shelves were
still wonky but they now looked shiny with
all the clocks sat atop them like shining
trophies. The windows now let the sunlight

through which in turn brightened up the
room making it now look inviting, the
floors were squeaky clean with the large
rug at the centre of the room now being
completely dust free. Thaddeus had one
more task which was to turn the Closed
sign to Open, something that had not been
done in months, he walked over to the door
and flipped the sign round but he had not
made it halfway back across the room
before he heard the bell on the shop door
ring out loudly. He turned and saw Mrs.
Bundleberry walking briskly through the
door with that same expression across her
face that Thaddeus saw just before he set
out on his and Takt's adventure, "Hello
Mrs. Bundleberry" Thaddeus said as he
rounded the counter and took a seat on the
creaky stool before looking up at the tall
Mrs. Bundleberry, he found it hard not to
smile now knowing that she was a
Spindlebock, a half spider half human
creature, "Hello Thaddeus, had a bit of
spring clean have we?" said Mrs.
Bundleberry as she peered down at him,
"Yes I have" said Thaddeus, "Hmmm" said
the Spindlebock, "It looks rather nice in
here, and you don't look too bad yourself"
she said with her posh voice with a hint
of a raspy hiss, and then Thaddeus saw a
slight smile crease her thin face, "What
can I do for you?" asked Thaddeus as he
smiled back, "It's my pocket watch, it
seems to have stopped working and the
hands seemed to be jammed, can I fix it

for me?" she asked, "I can indeed, it will
be ready tomorrow for you is that ok?"
asked Thaddeus as Mrs. Bundleberry handed
over the gold edged watch with its long
silver chain and as Thaddeus took it in
his hand he smiled with the memory of Takt
who was now sitting far back behind him in
the corner of the room and top of a
crooked old stool, "That will be fine"
said Mrs. Bundleberry" and as she turned
and started to walk back towards the door
she turned her head to partly look back at
Thaddeus, "Oh and another thing Thaddeus"
she started as Thaddeus looked away from
the pocket watch at her, "Well done in
finding the Todesfall Clock, you have made
this world a little safer for all of us"
and with that she smiled and exited the
shop, but as he walked off to the right
and down the street Thaddeus saw a figure
standing opposite the shop, the figure
stood all wrapped in a cloak on the other
side of the street. None of the passersby
noticed the stranger but Thaddeus thought
there was something familiar about the
figure, and then he saw a glimpse inside
the hood and at the slightly brown face
with large eyes peering at him, then the
figure extended a long arm from within the
cloak and waved at him but barely moving
the arm and instead just curling the
fingers of the long and thin hand.
Thaddeus saw the skin was also a deep
brown and looked almost like bark from a

tree but with crusted mud clinging to the palm of the hand.

Thaddeus stared at the figure who he now knew to be Bolgreena Mollhog, the Witch he and Takt had met at the Maug Lake and as the figure began to move he saw her smile and nod with which he returned an acknowledging nod before she walked away and out of Thaddeus' sight. Thaddeus smiled to himself at how his life now felt so much different, the journey had changed him in so many ways and the fact that he had seen his beloved wife Pandora and also Fadfin, Gideon and Takt, this made him happy as he had fought for something and in doing so he had realized his true self. He had realized what he was capable of and not only this, he had seen a world he had never thought had existed, a world that was right before him for all these years and he now wondered what more he would see in the coming years, would the mythical world he had stepped into along with his best friend Takt still be visible to him for the rest of his days? Thaddeus thought one thing was for sure and this was that he would always remember the world he had seen and he would always remember the adventures that life could bring.

Epilogue.

The battle was over and Feen Lowenzahn had returned from the fields outside of the home the Ink Twins once dwelt within. The tall Fairy King stood looking out upon the now quiet Fairy village, the Pixie hoard had been defeated and he had lost many Fairies but he was comforted at the thought that many Fairies survived, they had escaped into the village below and had begun the rebuilding of their homes within the dandelions.

The Pixie bodies had been disposed of and the dead Fairies were part of the Earth, waiting to be reborn within a sunflower. Feen exited the room that he had met with Thaddeus and Takt weeks previously and swiftly walked down the hallways of the Dandelion House, his long robes billowing behind him. He moved down the large staircase and then down the passageway that led to the room which would take the king into the dandelion stem. He moved down the stem, quickly stepping his large feet onto the moist steps. He moved past the opening where Fairies would take flight on dandelion seeds, he moved ever further down, past the storage leaf for the seeds and soon he came to the very bottom of the stem. He was now underground and was faced by a large cavern that had a giant door of bark at its head.

He moved forward and unlocked the door before pushing hard that then sounded an audible creak. Once inside the Fairy king was faced with a large cavernous room that was edged by giant boulders of dried dirt and mud, ivy and vines protruded the ceiling of the hollowed room and at its centre was a large, glistening pool of electric blue water.

Feen approached the pool which had a small crooked bridge at its centre, the bridge led to a small island that housed a pillar. Feen stepped before the pillar that had atop it the Moak Crone Pearl, the pearl was fastened tightly by metallic vines that were green in color but which constantly moved and tightened around the Pearl. Now that the Moak Crone Pearl was bonded with the rock that formed it, the Fairy world was safe and was finally hidden. Feen Lowenzahn stood looking at the Pearl before suddenly a noise sounded behind him, he spun quickly to find the source of the sound and saw a cloaked figure stood before the bridge. "Who are you? How did you get in here?" shouted Feen with his bellowing voice. "You know who I am Feen, have you forgotten your old friend?" said the stranger in a voice that sounded like air through clouds. The cloaked figure then removed the hood that shrouded his face and Feen saw that it was an Elf, the king of Elves, Aeilva Vancney. "Feen Lowenzahn, the Elves are in danger and we need your help".

Printed in Great Britain
by Amazon

67569750R00158